MW00580309

Caught Naked

By

Doug Weeks

Caught Naked

Copyright © 2023

Douglas Wesley Weeks

Aka Doug Weeks

All rights reserved.

ISBN: 978-1-7368813-2-3

They shaped this story.

This book wouldn't exist if it weren't for the corrections, suggestions, and encouragements of Peter Pullen and my good friend, Ken Lord, who also formatted the book and helped with its publication. Maria Singh and Paul and Kate Honess showed where I could cut the good that got in the way of the best in the story. Look at their name. Do you see hones and honest in Honess? They, along with the others, honestly honed this book. Jennifer Gooden drew my attention to people who are too sensitive or fragile to read books like this. My grandson, Rhett Cox, provided thoughtful criticism, and with my son by marriage, Will Thornton, helped with computer related problems, which were many. My eldest child, Reushann Cox, designed the cover. She also read the book aloud to me and caught implausible statements and actions, increasing the story's realism. Finally, I couldn't have dealt with the story's pain and harshness were it not for the encouraging support of my wife, Janeen. You, my editorial team, I hold in high regard with deep gratitude.

I introduce you now to Dave, the narrator, who can't wait for you to meet the people who have come to him in this fictional story, especially Heather, Krystyl, Ana, and Marta, who bristles a bit when people insist on calling her, Martha. These women are evidence that the One who made us knows how to remake us. And he specializes in the most impossibly broken.

Dedication

I had you in mind when this story came to me. I wanted to summon you to war against a hellish regime under which millions exist as slaves. I knew about sex trafficking, but it was merely another cause until someone conscripted me to write about the rescue of four sex-trafficked women, whom you'll meet in this fictional story. I hope you enter the lives of fellow human beings trapped in this loathsome condition, rescue as many as you can, and help rebuild their broken lives. Or perhaps our Commander recruited you to fight on another front. Your victory strengthens me, and mine encourages you. So, I dedicate this report to the warriors stationed on all fronts, including yours and mine.

"Let my heart be broken by the things that break the heart of God." Bob Pierce, founder of *World Vision*.

Stop! Read no further if....

If you or someone you love has been sexually abused and reading about sexual abuse could bring back painful memories that would cause further harm, don't read this book. I want this book to help people understand how what God created to bring us to the highest heights of pleasure can be manipulated to shatter us beneath the lowest depths of shame. You know enough about the dark, painful world of harmful sex. This book is not for you.

If you have succeeded in protecting yourself from the dark side of sex and you want to keep your thoughts free from descriptions of harmful ways sexuality can be used, don't read this book.

Finally, this book is also not good for the reader who doesn't intend to use this story to better understand and fight sexual exploitation. If you merely want to satisfy your curiosity about the selfish forms of sexual behavior, I hope you don't read this story. If you do, I hope this book will transform you just as key persons in this story are transformed into persons who hate what God hates about man's selfish use of the gift of sex. The main characters in this story learn to love what God loves about sex, i.e., the exclusive mutual surrender of a husband and wife to each other for the pleasure of pleasing one another.

If you want to join others in creating a safer world for at-risk women and children—a world that protects them from being captured, tortured, and enslaved, read on.

Foreword

Caught Naked by Douglas Wesley Weeks is a terrifyingly gripping fictional story of how a dedicated few can stir up a whole community to fight sexual predation. I found the book hard to put down. It provides plenty of opportunities for men and women to look at their attitudes toward this issue and provides a consistent Christian viewpoint toward reconciliation. The heroes of the story have fanciful skills in the use of firearms and in their ability to withstand physical punishment, but the author's development of the characters keeps us reading raptly through these passages. Recommended for Christians [and all] wishing to explore their stake in the battle against sexual exploitation of women and children.

James L. Greenwald, MD, Family Physician

Caught Naked goes viral!

It's possible. How?

Creative marketing can bring it to the attention of many. But the best sellers of this book will be you who read the book and enthusiastically tell your friends about it.

But be prepared for some pushback. You'll be telling your friends about a business that enslaves millions but remains mostly hidden because people, if they see it, don't want to deal with it, so they pretend not to see. I hope that you'll have the courage to take people beyond their comfort zone by challenging them to get involved at some level.

They may simply read and promote this book. Or they may investigate to uncover sexual exploitation in their area and follow the example of people in this story who find unique ways of combating sex trafficking. It's everywhere. It's entrenched. It's powerful. But it's not invincible. It's crucial that we act now. Every minute of delay adds to the suffering of those who can't deliver themselves from the hellish world they inhabit.

TABLE OF CONTENTS

1. "Help!" 1

2. Escape through the night.................................... 14

3. Up a creek without a paddle 20

4. Hidden, yet exposed... 23

5. The best-laid plans... 30

6. Who's tracking whom?....................................... 35

7. Fly Guy's web.. 38

8. Excruciating interrogation................................. 41

9. Focus on her eyes 44

10. What women should know about men 54

11. Mafia to free Heather? 57

12. Mac and Fly Guy flee 59

13. All but one saved from the fire 62

14. Carriage house hideout.................................... 70

15. Who can I trust? 77

16. Dawn visitors 88

17. Does anyone care? 99

18. Stunning by stunning 104

19. On the run.. 114

20. Skirting around an orgy................................... 121

21. Drug withdrawal.. 126

22. Celebration breakfast...................................... 130

23. The man every woman needs 133

24. Marta — The last time I cried 136

25. Krystyl — Satan's slave 139

26. Ana — Child seeking way home 145

27. Women: Re-creating 148

28. Men: fighting sex trafficking 151

29. Krystyl's battle with demons.............................154

30. Talk of rehab...158

31. Girls' untimely departure 160

32. Rescuer rescued...163

33. Jesus, friend of sluts 171

34. Vengeance? Hard to let it go.............................175

35. Jailed...181

36. Spy among us...188

37. Solitary = severe seduction 192

38. Thrown to the wolves 195

39. Escape from the prison clinic............................201

40. Home at last! 204

41. Abolition of Sexploitation 208

42. I fire my lawyer 216

43. Justice at last!...219

44. Memory of justice...222

45. Everyone loves a good story 226

Epilogue 245

Other books by Doug Weeks 267

Afterword 268

1. "Help!"

8:30 p.m. Sunday, April 1, 2018

The yellow missive, propelled by gusts of wind, sailed from a roadside trash pile, and stuck to my damp windshield long enough for me to read the word "Help!" before the wipers brushed it aside. I was about to do the same, brush it aside. But that hastily scribbled "Help!" snagged my mind, launching an internal debate:

Should I check this out?

Don't be ridiculous. It's just a bit of trash. Even if it had been an urgent appeal, the crisis would be over by now...

How do you know? Someone may be in trouble right now, and I am meant to help.

Curiosity, if not compassion, along with my thirst for risky escapades, won the debate. My career as a cop, before I retired, and my current work as a private investigator had not tamed my lust for adrenaline-pumping action. *Maybe this note is inviting me to a stimulating assignment.*

Waiting until the traffic cleared, I U-turned back to search for the paper. The night's moonless darkness, combined with the wind-driven swirling trash, reduced my ability to see as I poked around in the roadside rubbish. *How am I going to find one lonely piece of paper on this littered street? This is stupid.*

Then I saw it—the yellow paper with its pleading cry, "Help!" It was snagged on a nest of sticks that was being pushed by the wind toward a sewer grate. *Hold on!* I ran, bent down, and scooped it up just as the rushing wind carried its nest over the grate where gravity waited to suck it into the sewer's netherworld.

As I had imagined, the note contained more. I ran to my SUV, turned on the dome lights, and read: "Held captive. Save me. 3245 Dav…." The writing stopped short.

I began thinking of possible endings for "Dav"…*Davis, Davison, David, Davidson, Davenport Street, Avenue, Lane, Turnpike, Parkway. This could take forever. There must be a better way.*

The note probably came from someone near here who released it to the wind, hoping it would be carried into the hands of a kind person. What's the likelihood of that happening? Zilch. Is this a miracle? Oh, there's also the number of the house on some street starting with "Dav"….

My map showed Davison Street two blocks to the north. When I arrived, I discovered that the street lacked lighting, making it hard to read the house numbers, but I knew I was near when I deciphered 3225 Davison Street. *I need to get out and search on foot for 3245.*

I checked the pockets on the inside of my belt which held an unusually tiny cellphone. Another belt pocket carried my small tools for picking handcuff locks and other locks.

I clipped a can of pepper spray to my belt, locked the car, and began walking. *Being on foot beats finding house numbers from the car. The only problem is—I can't find a house numbered 3245 on Davison Street.*

I returned to the car to look at the map and found a "Davenport Street" six blocks to the south. It turned out to be even more poorly lit, featuring houses with boarded windows, sagging porches, and overgrown, trash-littered lawns. I began to wonder if I, David Von Moeller, a retired cop, and neophyte private investigator, should be sleuthing this neighborhood alone.

But I had a penchant for helping people in crisis. So, this cry for help hooked me. *At least, I should look.* I parked the car one street over from Davenport, locked it, and walked back to Davenport.

Decades earlier, when I had tried to get a few voyeuristic thrills, I had learned to make myself nearly invisible by sheltering in deep shadows, blending with the bushes, and freezing when the person I was pursuing looked in my direction. The idea was to remain unseen while seeing everything. Using these skills, I cased out 3245 Davenport. The incoming storm gave added cover, masking the sounds I made. The house seemed abandoned. No lights. Windows boarded up, from the front to the rear.

As I tried the back door, to see if it was unlocked, I heard footsteps approaching from inside. I scurried to hide behind a large oak near the house and waited, motionless. A board covered the back door's small window. *That knothole in the board probably serves as a peephole. Can he see me?* I waited and waited. At last, I slipped into the shadowy backyard.

Carefully avoiding sliding and falling in the mud of the grassless lawn, I wondered as I walked to the backyard's rickety fence. *Who would stay in such a decrepit dump? Probably junkies. Are they armed? What does it matter? Whoever wrote that note could be trapped in this wreck of a house. Shouldn't I at least try to find out?*

With curiosity rising, I planned my next move. *I can't go to the police without knowing what's going on in there.* I looked at the house, begging for a clue when I noticed a dark patch on the roof... *is that a hole?* Near the crumbling chimney was a hole big enough for a man to crawl through. A branch from a nearby tree hung right over it. *I can climb the tree, crawl out on the branch, and enter the house through that hole. But what if the roof around the hole is so rotten it gives way under my weight? Whoever is in there will hear me come crashing through the roof. Hmm. The roof ridge is straight. That means it can't be too decayed. I'll cling to the swaying branch until it swings near the ridge. Then I'll jump and grab the ridge, climb down from the ridge to the hole, and....*

The wind intensified, pounding the house, clawing at shingles, whistling through loose boards. *Even though it'll make holding onto that branch a rodeo ride, I hope it keeps up. I need this tempest to mask any noise I make.*

Anyone seeing my wavy, salt and peppered, shoulder-length hair and graying beard would have wondered how such an old man could be climbing so high up into a tree. The secret? Rigorous daily workouts. Even so, the trip up the tree winded me. So, I rested a minute before swinging hand over hand along the branch overhanging the roof. Because it swung so wildly, I gripped the branch tenaciously with each hand hold until I had propelled myself across to the ridge above the hole. I dropped, grabbing the ridge. The crumbling old shingles slid away under my feet, but the wood beneath stayed intact.

Before climbing down through the hole, I stuck my head in to see what was waiting for me in the attic. Risking being seen, I waited until my eyes adjusted to the attic's musky darkness. *Nobody here... or so it seems. And there's a floor, but this hole is so high above it that I'll have to drop a few feet.*

I squeezed through the hole feet first and dangled there until a blast of wind shook the house, hiding the sound of my fall to the attic floor. I found a narrow staircase that descended to the second floor. It squeaked, so I hesitated after each step, hoping the sound would blend with the ancient house's concert of groans and squeals.

When I reached the bottom step, I waited and listened, with my hand on the doorknob. Hearing no unusual movement, I eased open the door to a damp mildew-laden hallway on the second floor.

Again, I listened. *Can't hear anyone on this floor. Wait! Is that someone snoring?* To my right, stairs led down to the first floor. In front of me, four doors opened into a hallway. Although the storm created a continual rumble, I removed and carried my sneakers just to be sure no one could hear my footsteps. I peeked into each room. *Empty. Except for this room closest to the stairs.*

The snorer slept on his back with only a flimsy mattress between him and the floor. His beer belly formed a mound that filled the twin bed mattress. His limbs hung over the edges of the mattress, resting on the floor. *I hope he doesn't wake up before I get out of here. He's huge.*

I descended to the first floor where the stairs opened into a living room. Except for a couch and papers scattered around the room, the room was stripped bare—no pictures on the walls, not even boxes on the floor. I spied a yellow sheet of paper, like the one carrying the 'Help' message that had started me on this venture. *Hmm.*

I slipped into a small room adjoining the living room. It, too, was empty. Then there was the dining room—void of furnishings. In the kitchen, I found a skinny fellow, slouched in a chair at the table, sound asleep. Skirting around him, I came to the basement door. It stood open just far enough to allow me to maneuver around it without touching it. *I don't dare awaken that man with the sound of a squeaky door.* I descended to the basement where I slipped my sneakers back on.

In the center of the basement stood an ancient coal-burning furnace. Out of the upper part of the furnace, big round heat ducts snaked their way upward. *It looks like a giant hydra.*

I heard a weak moan. Following the sound to the furnace's back side, I discovered the source of the groan and gasped.

She couldn't have been older than sixteen. Not a stitch of clothing. Lying on her back on the concrete floor. Someone had shackled her wrists and ankles, stretching her arms and legs far apart in a spread-eagle position. Candles on either side of her prevented the darkness from hiding her nakedness. She probably thought I was one of them, because she struggled against the bonds, vainly trying to protect herself.

I ripped off my windbreaker and covered her. "I'm here to help you escape," I whispered. "Nod your head if you believe me."

She nodded and I removed her gag.

"How often do they come down," I whispered.

"Once an hour. Their next visit will be in about fifteen minutes."

"Who comes?"

"Just the one on duty. He comes to check on me and sometimes... it's so dirty. I can't... it hurts," she whispered.

"It's okay. You don't need to talk about it," I said.

I heard footsteps crossing the kitchen floor.

"I have to do this," I said as I replaced her gag and took my coat off from her. "Otherwise, they'll know someone's here. Don't worry. I won't let him hurt you."

The door to the basement opened wide, creaking as it swung on rusty hinges. As the man descended, I picked up a heavy board and hid in the coal bin. *If he decides to rape her, I'll knock him out with this hefty board.*

"You outshine all other women," his gravelly voice crowed. as the man came nearer the girl. "Irresistible, sexy, innocent....." He croaked his lewd song. "You'll make men dizzy with pleasure. Just need to tame you a bit." He unzipped his fly and....

You devil! I approached him from behind and brought the board crashing down on the back of his head. He slumped to the floor.

I took my rain slicker off and laid it over her, then removed her gag. From its pocket in my belt, I took the tool for unlocking handcuffs. "How long have they had you tied down?" I whispered as I worked on the first handcuff.

"Since this afternoon.... Before then, I thought Mac, the big guy, and Stanley, the guy you just clobbered, cared about me."

"How did you get here?"

"My stepdad dropped me off where all the whores operate. 'You belong here, you slut,' he said. Then he drove off.

"I was so lost, scared, and confused—hoping for someone to come and rescue me. Some street people saw me wandering. They seemed concerned for my safety and persuaded me to come to their home under a highway bridge. I should have stayed with them, but I wanted to find my way home before my stepdad came home from work. So, early the next morning, I headed in the direction that I thought would get me home. I found French fries in the trash. They tasted awful, but I was starving. I was scavenging for more scraps when a big man and his skinny friend came up....."

"Let me guess," I said as I freed one hand and started on the other. "The big man and his skinny sidekick offered to help you."

"Right. They gave me food and let me sleep on their couch."

Having released both hands, I worked on the cuff holding her right ankle.

"They were both in the kitchen," the girl said. "They must have thought I was asleep. I heard them talking about how much they would make selling me to their customers. I freaked. I had to escape."

"Is that when you made that 'Help!' sign?" I asked as I freed her right foot.

"Yeah. I had a pen in my shirt pocket. I found a piece of yellow paper from the litter on the floor and wrote that cry for help. A window was open enough for me to get my hand through, and I let go of the note when I felt the wind tugging at it."

"I want to hear the rest of your story, but right now, we need to get out of here." Freeing her left foot, I helped her get to her feet. The slicker that had covered her, slid off, so I held it for her to get into. It came down to her knees. She looked ridiculous. I smiled. A slight quiver at the corners of her mouth told me she wanted to smile but couldn't.

I rolled up her sleeves, so I could see her hands. "Let's see if you can walk." Leaning on me, she walked around the furnace. At first, she was wobbly, but gradually her strength returned. "Are you ready to go?" I asked.

She nodded.

"If someone tries to stop us, I'll take care of him. You run to the fire station, next to McDonald's, which you can see from the front of this house. Let's go." We ascended the stairs and tiptoed through the kitchen to the back door, which let us out onto the back porch.

"Where the hell do you think you're going?" A voice boomed from the kitchen.

"Run!" I yelled, shoving her through the door. And she ran.

I placed myself between the big man and the girl, facing the muzzle of the big man's semi-automatic. He was almost seven feet tall!

"You've got some explaining to do." He waved me into the house with his weapon and told me to sit at the kitchen table. "Like what did you do with Stanley?"

"I'm here, Mac," said a voice from the basement stairway. As he ascended, he continued, "I was about to give the girl the treatment, when someone hit me from behind. When I woke up, the girl was gone." Stanley saw me sitting at the table. "So, you're the one who clubbed me?" He felt the back of his head gingerly.

I didn't respond.

"Answer Stanley or I'll shut you up for good." Big Mac held his pistol at my throat.

Sweat coursed down my back. I was in alarm mode. *This bully's appetite for terrorizing people is voracious. But I'm not going to satisfy him.* So, I answered nonchalantly. "Yes, I stopped you, Stanley." *Maybe I should act as if I were one of them.* "You took my girl," I said. "I was just protecting my property. I don't take kindly to anyone giving 'the treatment,' as you call it, to any of my girls."

"Hah, you don't fool me. She's not your girl. You're working for the police," Mac said.

"Then why aren't they here backing me up and busting you folks? They wouldn't put one of their own in this kind of situation without backup."

"So, who are you? Good cop? Bad cop? Wannabe pimp? It doesn't matter. The girl is mine," Mac roared. "I'll get her buh, buh, back." Mac's roar was reduced to stuttering gasps as his eyes fixed on to something behind me.

I turned and saw nothing but a coal black cat.

Trembling, Mac screamed, "Stanley, you left the basement window open again. Now, get that thing out of here and lock the window." Mac repeated unintelligible phrases, then became catatonic.

He's scared of a cat! I sat in silence, biting my tongue, and glaring with contempt as I looked at him from head to toe. "You sound way too cocky for a small-time operator. What makes you so sure you'll get the girl back?"

"Idiot! Nothing happens in this hood if I don't let it, including this." He struck me across the face with the back of his huge hand. "You have released the little girl into my turf. That makes her mine. Our people will get her back, even if the cops have her," the big man boasted. "Now I want to know, what's your game? Who are you working with? How did you find out about us?"

"Everyone on the streets is talking about you." I exaggerated to stroke his ego. "'Don't mess with that giant,' they're warning everyone. But you're only a small-time operator if you have to ask who I am."

My delight in putting the narcissist in his place made the second blow to my face worth it. But hoping to speed things along, I decided to cooperate and answer his questions. "I don't shine anyone's shoes but my own. Solo is my game, but I have friends, including capos in the West Wend Mafia."

"Capos?" Mac muttered.

"Capo is short for *caporegime*, the rank just below a Mafia underboss," I said. "Capos head the teams that do the work the Mafia wants done. How do you not know this?"

"Ha-ha! Friends in the Mafia? Sure, I bet you do. Yeah, just like we have friends in the police force." Mac looked at Stanley and both men burst into laughter.

They obviously knew nothing about the local Mafia. I figured my story was plausible, and to keep them guessing, I added, "As for how I got in here... you need to fix your roof."

"So, you came in through the hole in the roof? And got to the basement without waking us. Not bad."

"Yeah, and you shake the house when you snore, big man."

Mac grunted.

I turned to the skinny guy. "How you sleep so soundly slouched in a kitchen chair baffles me. I could have tied you to the chair while you slept, you sorry watchdog. And you might want to zip up your fly, guy."

He looked down. Sure enough.

"Lock him up, Stanley," the big man ordered. "I might find some use for him before we make him disappear."

Good news: my bravado has bought me time. Bad news: if I can't escape, they'll kill me.

As the skinny guy with the narrow, hooked nose led me down the stairs, my hands were busy behind me. I took the handcuff tool from its pocket in my belt and squeezed it between my pinky and ring finger.

"Take everything off." I did, except for socks and underwear.

"Lie down on your back with your head here." He pointed at a slight depression in the concrete floor.

Having cuffed me in a spread-eagled position on my back, my captor deposited my clothes in the coal bin. He returned to kick me in the groin and laughed as I uselessly tried to double over. "I liked that so much I think I'll do it again." He slammed his boot into my groin with even more force. It took all my might to keep from crying out, but I was determined not to give him that pleasure. Sweat trickled from my forehead down my neck.

As I lay writhing on the cold concrete floor, I wondered, *Are the girls we view in porn trained by treatments like those Mac and Fly Guy use? How dare we take part in such soul-destructive training?* It struck me that this girl was probably the same age as my sixteen-year-old daughter. *What if these perverts captured Jenna?* A flash of fury raged through me. I could hear my sweat sizzling as it dripped from my body to puddle on the cold concrete.

2. Escape Through the Night

10:30 p.m. Sunday, April 1

With my arms spread wide, I couldn't bring my hands together to pick the lock. *Should I try to do this with one hand? God, help! I've never tried this.*

I imagined God chuckling, "Don't you think I know you've never done this? Still, it won't hurt to try."

I turned my palm upward, so if, God forbid, the tool fell, it would fall into my palm, from which I might be able to retrieve it. Gradually, I slid the tool from its hiding place between my pinky and ring fingers. *Oops, I almost dropped it. Lord, have mercy.*

It took about fifteen minutes to maneuver the hand-cuff-picking tool to between my thumb and index finger. But try as I might, I couldn't find the correct angle to insert the tool into the lock. My fingers trembled, cold, clammy sweat made them slippery, and what I feared came to pass. I dropped the tool. *This is never going to work.... Shut up, you pessimistic Puddleglum. It's got to work or you're dead.*

Fortunately, the tool landed in my palm, and I maneuvered it so that it was again between my thumb and index finger. But I still couldn't find the correct angle. Then heaven came to my aid. Moon rays shining through the basement window illuminated the key to my deliverance. I noticed a crack in the concrete beneath my hand. *What if I anchor the tool in the crack?*

14

Could I position the hole of the cuff lock over the tool, insert it, and maneuver the handcuffs, so that the tool snaps the cuff lock open?

Somehow, I successfully anchored the tool in the crack and positioned the hole of the cuff lock over the tool, so the tool went down into the lock. After twisting and turning my wrist several times, click! The cuff opened.

I had just unlocked my other hand when I heard footsteps coming toward the basement stairs. *I'm going to have to pretend my wrists are still shackled and hope they don't inspect too closely.*

"Thought I'd come down and pay you a courtesy call." Fly Guy landed another kick to my groin. Little did he know that I was struggling not to get out of the handcuffs, but to stay in them. I desperately wanted to grab his foot and break his ankle.

"It's okay to cry if you want. Big boys do cry," he mocked.

"I'll die first, your sadist."

He stood silhouetted between me and the window, so I couldn't make out his facial expression, but it must've been angry, because he kicked me again, this time in the ribs. *When am I going to learn to control my tongue? It earns me so much pain.*

Fly Guy sneered, then went back upstairs, slamming the door as he went.

I waited, doubled over. As my throbbing pain slowly diminished, I heard him settle in his chair. My gut and groin groaned. I wanted to roll up in a fetal position, but danger demanded action. So, I picked the locks on my feet, stood, shook my legs and arms, and took deep breaths to try to relieve the extraordinary pain in my gut and chest. In the coal bin, I found my clothes and dressed.

I tested the basement window. *It opens. And its hinges allow me to remove it.* I removed the window, carried a crate to the wall beneath the window, climbed up on the crate, and out the window. I retreated to the backyard and looked back at the house. *Good, all is quiet.* I climbed over the decrepit back fence and went through the neighbor's yard to the street where I had parked my car.

It's gone! I should've known better than to park it on a backstreet in this neighborhood. Hidden in the shadow of a yew tree, I looked for the most shadowed path to the fire department.

Vandals had smashed at least half of the streetlights, probably using them for target practice, but enough streetlights remained to cast shadows. Darting to the shadows of bush, tree, and building, I waited in each shadow until the coast was clear to run to the next shaded area. I finally arrived across the street from the fire station.

Hmm... two police cars. Mac's comment about having friends with the police made me wonder. *Does Mac have both the Police and Fire Department in his hand? If so, I can't mention the girl, or they'll hand me back over to Mac. But I can mention my stolen car and hope they don't connect that with me, Mac's intruder. I'll just have to take my chances.*

Except for a few cars prowling the neighborhood, a ghostly emptiness haunted the street. I waited until the cars were out of sight, then crossed the street and stealthily entered the fire station.

The conversation I overheard as I stood in the entryway infuriated and frightened me:

"The girl came to us dressed in nothing but a man's jacket," one of them said. "We turned her back over to Mac."

How could they? I fumed as I exited.

The fire station cast a deep shadow over the vacant lot beside it. Hidden by that shadow, I walked through the littered lot to the back of the fire station, where, to my surprise, I found a firefighter tied and gagged. By his wrinkled brow, I guessed he was about fifty. *I'll bet he's on my side.* The man confirmed my thoughts when I removed his gag.

"Hide behind the dumpsters," he said. "They're coming now."

I started to retie his gag, but he bit my hand. "No time for that. Hurry."

I barely got behind the dumpsters when a cop and the fire chief came out the back door. I watched through the space between the dumpsters. "What did you decide, Ron?" the fire chief asked.

"You all disgust me. I'll have nothing to do with ruining that girl."

"Hey, you Black son of a bitch, how did you get your gag off?" The cop held his pistol to the older man's head.

The older man grinned.

"Not funny, idiot." The cop backhanded the man.

"You don't want to get hurt." The fire chief firmly brushed the cop aside. "And we don't want to hurt you. We'll give you a half hour more to make your final decision. Think of your wife and kids."

"I've already made....."

As if he didn't want Ron to seal his doom by saying too much, the fire chief shoved the gag into Ron's mouth and tightly tied it. Then he and the police officer went back inside.

I ran from the dumpster to untie the ropes around Ron's feet and hands. I began to rub his ankles to improve circulation.

"No time for that. Follow me," he urged as he started running down the firehouse alley.

I followed close behind with the adrenaline of urgency kicking in.

After about five hundred yards, Ron turned north and kept running another five hundred yards. We came to a creek, swollen by the rain. It must have been fifteen feet wide. In the distance, I heard the baying of hounds. *Could they be chasing us already?*

"Can you swim?" Ron asked.

"Like a fish."

"Good, the creek gets narrow and deep in a few places."

We ran downstream on the path alongside the creek. Then Ron reversed directions and began running backward upstream. Why upstream?" I asked.

"Upstream, a recently built police community center has a hideout we can use until we've planned our next move," Ron said.

"Why run backward?" I asked.

"We want all the footprints to point downstream so people searching for us think that is the direction we're going."

Just before we reached the spot where we had begun our deceptive detour, Ron jumped into the creek and began wading upstream. I followed.

"The water will wash away all traces of our going upstream," Ron said. "If they go downstream for a half hour before they turn around, we'll be a half-mile upstream where it'll be safer to get out."

"I got to hand it to you, Ron." I reached over and punched his shoulder. "You know what you're doing and where you're going. I don't mind admitting I'm lost."

3. Up a Creek Without a Paddle

2 a.m., Monday, April 2

We battled a stream made treacherous by shifting currents, stumbling over rocks, and tripping over tree limbs. After an hour, penetrating pain stiffened my legs. "Can we get out and rest on the bank?" I asked.

"It's taking much longer than I had thought to get upstream. The dogs... do you hear them? It sounds like they're getting closer. That means we need to get to that substation."

As we pressed on, I told Ron how a cop and the fire chief had returned the girl I had rescued to Mac. "Can you believe it?" I asked.

"I knew the chief had done some shady things recently," Ron said, "but it's hard to believe he'd stoop that low." We lapsed into silence as we swam, waded, and stumbled upstream.

I couldn't get that girl off my mind. *What are Mac and Fly Guy doing to her now?* Finally, I blurted out, "I hate people like Mac and everyone he's tied to. They're predators... like a pack of wolves chasing down a defenseless doe. How can they do it?" I asked Ron. The question had pursued me since my early days on the police force.

"Well," Ron began and then paused. "Do you want the deep psychological approach of Dostoyevsky's *Crime and Punishment...* or the journalistic approach of Truman Capote's *In Cold Blood*," he asked with a raised eyebrow and tilted head.

"I don't mean to belittle these great writer-philosophers, but they aren't enough," I said. "In my line of work, I see the tragic devastation of evil men and women up close every day."

"And they raise questions for which no one has given a satisfying answer," Ron said. "The questions rise again tomorrow, just as soul-searching and scary as ever."

Precisely. I thought. *For the first time, I've found someone who understands.*

"It's a great topic for later...," Ron said, "but we're still up a creek without a paddle."

I chuckled at his lighthearted description of our serious dilemma. *He's alright. I like him.*

Ron pointed out a tree up ahead with massive branches that overspread the creek. "See how the tip of that branch dips into the creek, from where it goes almost straight up, and then curves over to the main trunk? The dogs, if they come up this far, will be sniffing along the banks of the creek for our exit place...."

"I get it," I said. "We won't exit by climbing up the creek bank where the dogs will be sniffing. Instead, we'll climb up that branch from the middle of the creek. We can go on that branch to the tree trunk which will let us down fifteen feet from where the dogs will be sniffing along the creek bank."

Ron went first. "I don't think the police hounds will pick up our scent this far away from the creek bank," Ron said, as we alighted from the tree.

"Mac's guys might be watching my home to catch me when I return. Or they could be checking my home phone," Ron said, mentally checking things off a list as he headed toward the community center. "So, we can't call there. We've had our cell phones off just in case they have techies that could somehow track us... By the way, my full name is Ron Fox. And yours...?

"Von Moeller, David Von Moeller," I said.

"Do you have trustworthy family or friends you could call, using the police community center phone?"

"My wife, sixteen-year-old daughter, cousin... that's it."

"Do you think your wife called the police to report you missing?"

"We've agreed that she won't report me missing until we've lost contact for two days. That keeps her from interrupting when I'm on a time-sensitive part of a case," I said. "I am a retired cop, and now, to keep mentally alert, I dabble in private investigative work."

"So, we can safely use the police substation phone to call your wife."

"But what about you, Ron?" I asked. "How can you go back to work. You know too much about the fire chief's involvement in sex trafficking."

"Until last night, I would have sworn that no one in the Fire Department was connected with that sordid business," Ron said. "I'm not sure what to do, but I'm not going home until I know I won't put my family at risk."

Ron stopped in front of an old warehouse recently converted into a police-sponsored community center. "Here's the substation I mentioned."

4. Hidden, Yet Exposed

4:30 a.m. Monday, April 2

"Do you guys realize what you're into?" The questioner, Al, locked the community center's two doors as we entered. "I'm supposed to keep this place open twenty-four seven, but I can't risk anyone overhearing what we have to say."

Even though Al had locked the doors, he spoke in hushed tones. "Selling sex has become big business in West Wend. The sex industry has bought off or frightened a sizable part of the police department. Only a few, like me, stand up to oppose it. And for that we get harassed and spied on. Still, I'm probably overly cautious to lock us in here. After all, who is going to spy on us at four-thirty in the morning?"

The words were hardly out of his mouth when someone began pounding on the door. Al pointed to the computer room. "There's a hideout behind the back wall of the closet in that room. The latch is in the upper right corner. Go!"

While we worked on opening the fake wall, I heard Al enter the bathroom. He stayed awhile, flushed the toilet, came out, and walked slowly to answer the door.

Good delaying tactics, Al.

I heard a bullying voice saying, "Aren't you supposed to keep this center open?"

"My partner took sick and had to go home. So, I locked the doors while I was using the crapper."

Good story, Al.

"What brings you two barging into my turf at four thirty in the morning?" Al demanded.

"We're looking for two fugitives," a high-pitched, snooty voice responded.

"We have orders to search this place, and that's what we plan to do," a bullying voice added.

Ron and I had opened the fake wall and climbed inside the hideout.

"Not so fast!" Al said, stalling for valuable time while Ron and I struggled to close the false wall.

Mr. Snooty High Voice must have heard our struggle. "I'm going to check out the back room," he said. We could hear him walking toward the computer room where we were still struggling to close the panel.

"Hey, buddy!" Al barked. "Get back here and follow protocol. You may be wearing police uniforms, but that doesn't give you license to trample over a fellow cop. I need to see your credentials and badges."

Al took his time examining their papers and badges. But he didn't challenge them. "Go ahead. Look."

Ron and I had just closed the fake wall when we heard someone rush to open the computer room door.

God, make the tiny latch invisible.

Five minutes later he appeared from the room muttering, "No one in there. I could have sworn I heard someone in the computer room."

The other cop reported seeing no one also.

"What do they look like?" Al asked.

"One is fifty-three. Black. Bald, with gray hair on the sides. Five-foot-six. He's a city firefighter. His name is Ron. The other is white, about six-foot-three. He could be anywhere from forty to sixty. Name unknown."

"We had two guys here around five o' clock yesterday morning who answered that description," Al said. "They wanted directions to the nearest all-night restaurant. I told them about the truck stop two exits to the north on the interstate."

"Thanks," the bully muttered. "We'll check it out."

"Who's in charge of the investigation?" Al asked. "I need to know whom to report to if I see these guys again."

Ron and I heard them open the door to leave as an arrogant, high-pitched voice answered, "Chief Alexander."

The police chief? My shoulders tightened. *This is scary... Are we involved in something that reaches all the way up to him?* "I need to sit down," I said.

We had been standing with our ears glued to the wall, listening in on Al's conversation with the police officers. Add to that our hike up the creek. No wonder my legs were cramping.

Ron felt around in the dark and found two folding chairs. "Take a seat," he whispered. "We don't know how long it will be before it's safe for us to come out."

I had rested in the chair for barely a minute when the gloomy darkness unsettled me. "It sure would be nice to be able to see," I said. I stood and ran my hands over the walls, hoping to find a light switch. Nothing! Three of the walls were bare. A bookcase occupied part of the fourth wall.

"Did you feel behind the books?" Ron asked.

"No. Good idea."

We began taking down books and feeling behind them. *There's got to be light for reading these books.* Working quietly, we took down, felt behind, and then re-stacked the books. We had done this on two shelves and were about to give up when I pulled a large book from the third shelf—voila! We could see. Behind the book, I found a plunger switch like the switch on a refrigerator door. The book had held the plunger in the off position. When I removed the book, the switch released itself to the on position.

We heard muffled voices filter through the wall from outside. *Must be neighborhood visitors on their way to work.* I imagined life outside our box—people rushing to work, the sun rising and casting long shadows while burning off puddles from last night's rain.

My claustrophobic tendencies alerted me to how that sliver of a room crowded us. It was stuffy, too. Three times, I barely stifled a sneeze. *We can't betray our hiding place. But how long can we endure this?* We'd been in the room at least an hour and a half when Al finally entered. "Sorry, but I don't dare let you out. We are under surveillance. And it's a serious stakeout. They've got a drone circling above us and two strangers looking our way from the park across the street."

He paused. He must have noticed my breath coming in quick shallow pants. "Oh, I forgot to tell you how to get fresh air. Pull down volumes 22 through 25 of Encyclopedia Britannica and you'll find a vent."

Al didn't think to tell us about the light switch and the vent. I wonder what other convenience he has neglected to tell us about.

"I'm off duty in thirty minutes... at six. We'll plan our next move then, that is, if the coast is clear," Al continued. "I'll tell the two officers on duty today that you're here. You can count on them to be helpful. In the closet beside the bookcase, you'll find mats to sleep on, a stash of granola bars and other snacks, hand sanitizers, and urinals."

I misjudged you, Al. You do remember important details. Like urinals. I was wondering how much longer I could hold it.

After Al left, we hurriedly extracted the Britannica volumes that covered the air vent and took a long breath of early morning air.

"I know he doesn't want us to be caught." I flipped the pages of Britannica's volume 7, "But I don't know how long I can stay cooped up in this box."

"Have you heard of Henry 'Box' Brown?" Ron's whisper registered frustration, if not anger, as he grabbed my shoulders.

"Can't say that I have."

"Henry had friends ship him in a three-foot-by-two-foot crate to abolitionists in the north. He bumped along upside down for days in pain so extreme he thought he would die, all to be free.

"I guess what we've got here is a mansion compared to Henry's box," I said. "Forgive my whining. I should get my mind off myself and pray for the girl we're hoping to save from a hellhole worse than Henry's box."

"Let's not just talk about praying. Let's do it," Ron said.

Ron and I, in whispered appeals, 'stormed the towers of heaven' as Ron put it. We thanked God for choosing us to help this girl, and for guiding us. "Show us the next step... and the next... we believe you will."

I thanked God for showing me once again, how evil it was for men to use girls and women as toys for their pleasure. "Forgive me, Father, for my part in this evil game—checking them out, wanting their bodies, lusting," I confessed. "I may not be doing what Mac and Fly Guy are doing, but I'm thinking along the same lines when I let lust enter."

"What are you saying?" Ron interrupted. "We're nothing like those guys. They're exploiting women, dominating them, enslaving them, destroying them. We're not doing that. We're trying to stop their abuse."

"True," I said. "But when I fall into lusting, even if it's only thoughts, I'm heading the same direction as Mac and Fly Guy."

"Okay, now I'm hearing you. You're not saying it's wrong to appreciate a woman's beauty, right?" Ron asked.

"Right. But in no way should I isolate her beauty from all that she is, thinking of physical attractiveness only. I want to see her as a whole person."

"To be honest, I often focus on a woman's physical appeal and don't appreciate her other more important qualities," Ron said.

"I struggle with the same temptation," I said.

5. The Best-laid Plans...

6:30 a.m.—7:30 p.m., Monday, April 2

"I've heard bits of info about how you got caught up in rescuing this teenager," Ron said. "What's the full story?"

I recounted all that had happened to me that night, from the "Help" note on my windshield to my meeting Ron behind the fire station.

"That's where you come in." I spoke. "You know the rest of the story; except you'll never know how grateful I am for the way you got us safely to this tiny hide out."

We lapsed into our private thoughts, stunned by the circumstances we had been thrown into.

Ron's whisper broke the silence. "How did Mac get so much power around here?"

"Especially over the police and firemen!" I said.

"Maybe they're part of the Mafia," Ron suggested.

"Can you see a fat slob like Mac being a caporegime?" I asked.

"A capo...what?" Ron questioned.

"Caporegime. It's the name the Mafia uses for guys, not at the top, but near the top. The West Wend's small Mafia family keeps a low profile, but they have at least three caporegimes.

Here in West Wend they do the Mafia's legal and administrative tasks."

"How do you know so much about the Mafia?" Ron asked.

"They came up in different cases I worked on when I was a cop. I found them to be clever and careful. They, at least the West Wenders, were experts at going unnoticed."

"Is that why you doubt that Mac would be part of the Mafia?"

"Yeah," I said.

"So, Mac's control over this part of the city has nothing to do with the Mafia," Ron said. "We may never know how he muscled his way in. One thing we do know; he's not worried about the risks involved in being a renegade outlaw."

"By abducting this teen girl into sexual slavery, Mac and Fly Guy risk imprisonment for kidnapping, child endangerment, rape, prostitution, and other crimes.

"But even Mac has a limit to the amount of risk he'll take. I hope to push him beyond that limit," I said.

"How?" Ron asked.

"I haven't worked out the details." I took the pose of *The Thinker* with my elbow on my knee and my chin resting in my hand. "My point is that we must increase the risk of sex-trafficking while reducing its profit. If we scare Mac into thinking the Mafia is about to destroy him (which is likely), we make his business here too risky. If we get the IRS to come after him for unreported income, we cut into his profits. High risk. Low profit. Bye sexploitation."

"That makes sense," Ron said. "But it's hard to believe it can be done."

"Because it's impossible, should we not attempt it?"

We spent the rest of the day discussing my question, sleeping, swapping stories, and trying to figure out what to do next.

"What makes my blood boil is the involvement of the police and firemen in this cruelty," I said.

"I'm with you there."

"Think about it! Firefighters! The ultimate helpers of needy people, turned that girl over to a beast like Mac." The heat of anger rose from my chest to my face.

"They Dred Scotted her."

"What?" I questioned with my right eyebrow raised. "Is this another lesson from Black History?" Throughout the day Ron had been inspiring me with stories of Black people who had won their freedom, and the freedom of others at great cost. They fought for justice against impossible odds, and through amazing grace had forgiven their oppressors.

"Yeah. I'm taking you through Black History 101," Ron winked. Then he stood straight and ordered, "Get out your notebooks students and record this for your descendants." Ron spoke sternly but couldn't hide a grin.

"After living in a state that accepted him as a free man, Dred Scott was taken by his 'owners' back into territory that endorsed slavery. He sued for freedom for his family and himself on the grounds that he had been free while living in the free state. The courts ruled against him up to the Supreme Court, saying the U.S. Constitution did not apply to slaves. Slaves had no rights because they weren't U. S. citizens, but instead were the property of their owners. So, they turned Scott and his family over to their former owners to be enslaved again. This ruling was considered cruel and unjust by a growing number of Americans and led to the emancipation of slaves in the decade following the Dred Scott decision."

"So, our girl, having been freed, was Dred Scotted— returned to slavery," I said.

"How cruel! ... back then. And it's cruel now," Ron said.

"I can't chase out of my head images of that girl spread-eagled and abused by those filthy men. You know... It took a war to free slaves back then. Will freeing sex slaves demand anything less now?"

"You're on to something." Ron nodded vigorously. "What we need is a coordinated, all-out international war. Instead, we only go through isolated skirmishes, which, if won, benefit a few but leave the rest unprotected."

"We need a groundswell of Americans stirred up enough to go to war and stay at war until we consistently increase the risks and make the costs of illegal sex unprofitable for all involved," I said, as ideas that had been incubating were now pecking their way out of the shell.

"I'm impressed, Dave." Ron threw me a fist bump.

"But right now, there's a young girl who needs our help," I said, "so let's focus on the plan we've made to resolve her problems." At that moment, we heard a knock on the panel. It was Al's signal that he had come back on duty and wanted to talk.

"So, what's your plan?" Al asked.

"We need a distraction somewhere outside to give us a better chance of being undetected," I said. "I will leave from the front door, Ron from the rear. If one of us is caught, perhaps the other will escape."

"And if I escape unnoticed, I'll get what I need for a disguise, so I can move around unrecognized," Ron said. "I'll tell two of my trusted fire-fighting friends about the girl we're trying to rescue from sex traffickers. I'll ask them to explain to people who miss me at work that I'm on a special assignment. And, for sure, I'll inform Dave's and my family. That way, if they catch and silence Dave or me, you'll have people who, along with you, can counter any false allegations."

"Al, you could help by making a list of police officers we should avoid," I added. "And we need to know trustworthy officers whose help we can count on when we rescue the young girl."

"You said you needed something to hide your exit from here. Well, I think I've got the perfect distraction," Al said. "Our girls' volleyball team celebrates its winning of the city championship at seven o'clock tonight— an hour from now. We'll pack this place out—a perfect cover for you to slip away. I'll signal you when it's the right time."

6. Who's Tracking Whom?

8:30 p.m., Monday, April, 2

Everyone was too busy playing or watching volleyball, eating, or talking with friends, to notice Ron and I emerge from the closet in the computer room... or so it seemed. Added to the anonymity of being lost in the crowd, nightfall gave us the cover of darkness. As I walked beyond the outer fringes of the party and turned back to make sure no one was following, relief untangled the knots in my shoulders. I didn't realize how anxious I'd been.

Snap! The sound came from the tall bushes between me and the neighborhood merrymakers. I scanned the bushes in frozen silence... nothing.... I turned, ready to run when I saw a flash of movement. *No! It can't be.* Highlighted by the lights that illumined the outdoor volleyball courts was the silhouette of Fly Guy.

Should I run and shake him off? Should I attack? Not smart. He's probably got a gun. Should I at least try to circle and come up on him from behind? I opted for the circling maneuver.

I sprinted as fast as I could, much faster than he could run. He tried to equalize the race by shooting at me. A bullet grazed my leg. *He means business.* I ducked into a dark cemetery where only the faint light of the new moon could give away my position.

Tall tombstones provided shields as I zigzagged from one stone to another. But the zigzagging allowed Fly Guy to gain on me, so I ran on the path. *I'm risking his seeing me, but also increasing the distance between us.* Fly Guy kept shooting and missing. When I was about five hundred feet ahead and out of his sight, I ducked into a gully to the left of the beaten trail. Hiding behind the lower branches of a pine, I waited. *It worked!* Fly Guy stuck to the trail, ignoring the gully with its guardian pine.

The temptation to flee fought against the fact that I couldn't escape dealing with Fly Guy. He wasn't giving up.

I hate climbing pines. Their sticky sap takes forever to wash off. Besides, someone in a tree is an easy target, especially if he's six-foot-three. So, it's stupid for me to climb a pine when I'm a target and the ammo is live. But my murderous pursuer had slipped out of sight over a hill, so I climbed the pine to see which direction Fly Guy was going. To my surprise, he headed back toward me. As he came into view, I froze, not allowing any movement to betray my location.

As he approached the gully, he must have seen some twigs I bent or a fresh footprint in the moist dirt. *Kudos for his tracking skills. I guess he does have some smarts, after all. Dang it!* Fly Guy began investigating the gully.

Not bad, I thought, *they will find my body where dead bodies belong. How ironic!* I prayed two prayers: don't let him look up and let him pass beneath me. He picked up a long stick and began poking in the brush on each side of the gully. *He's taking forever.*

Sweat almost squirted from my arm pits and ran down my sides. At last, he passed beneath me. I jumped, landing on his back with a chop to the base of his skull. He went limp. *Oh no, I've killed him.* I checked his pulse. *Regular. He's breathing normally. Thank God!*

I examined him carefully, emptying his pockets. I removed his pistol, which I pocketed along with his wallet and cell phone. Everything else, I buried. I waited for him to wake up, planning to follow him and see where he would lead me. *I should be contacting my family, but I can't desert that teen girl who might not have any family seeking to rescue her.* So, I waited behind a huge oak.

At last, he woke, rubbed the back of his head, checked his pockets, and looked for his cell phone, wallet, and pistol. "Damn, he stole everything," he groused.

As if he hadn't planned to take everything from me, including my life. Following him was easy. He never looked back. *He must think I'm gone. Or he's leading me into a trap.*

7. Fly Guy's Web

9:30 p.m., Monday, April 2

Ask any fly who has encountered a spider's web and he will tell you the best traps keep you feeling free until long after you've been inescapably ensnared. To my chagrin, shame, and exasperation, I let Fly Guy lead me into a prize-winning trap.

Chagrin? I should have known he was making it too easy for me to follow him. When he turned around to face me with that menacing grin, I knew he had outwitted me. Three armed men surrounded me— that's chagrin.

Shame? When the teenaged girl I had promised to set free saw me as helpless as she, the dismay written on her face made it impossible for me to look her in the eye.

Exasperation? All our efforts had only made matters worse.

Fly Guy had led me to Mac's 'headquarters,' a stone and brick mansion tucked in a woodlot on the edge of town, invisible from the road. I hoped Ron had not fallen into a trap like I had. *Where are you, Ron? Did you escape or were you recaptured? If you escaped, did you find a way to tell our families...?*

#

I had slowed my pace, surprised by the opulence of this location contrasted to the stripped-bare hovel with a hole in the roof where Fly Guy and Mac had held me captive. *Was the other place a kind of jail for staff or customers headed toward execution or torture?*

38

Fly Guy cut my speculations short as he twisted my arm and shoved me through the first-floor office and sales area, which featured sensuous displays of spa and massage services, adult videos, adult books, and adult toys. *Adult? What a misnomer! Better labeled fools' toys.*

Years earlier, I had visited such places out of curiosity, which swiftly led to sexual addiction. Even though Jesus had delivered me from that addiction, and I hadn't frequented such places for thirty years, I felt the same intensity of craving as I did back then. I felt the same rush — that combination of extreme physical longing with mental confusion, and spiritual blackout.

A choir of voices flooded my mind, chanting: 'Just one look. Just one look.' Then I remembered how Ron and I had said our eyes need to be fixed on our wives only. So, I put my head down and avoided the 'scenery' crowding in on me.

Fly Guy's rough twisting of my arm and shoving me up the curved staircase to the second floor, supplied added help in guarding my eyes by reminding me of the painful outcome of yielding to sexual temptations.

Bedrooms that rarely provided rest occupied the second floor. The cleaning lady exited from one. As she maneuvered her cart, loaded with cleaning supplies, she left the door open long enough for me to see what looked like a bridal suite. *Hmm, they mock marital bliss while mimicking it. What a perversion of the faithful, permanent love that we grow into in Christian marriage. Instead of sex for a lifetime in which we learn, not merely the ABC's of sexual relationships, but their XYZ's (extra years of zest).*

We climbed to the third floor, a huge attic. One side had four stand-alone 'rooms.'

The other half of the attic was a wide-open space. At the far end of this open half of the attic, I noticed a mound, toward which Fly Guy shoved me. As I toppled onto the floor, I saw that the mound was the girl.

"I'm so sorry," I began, as I looked at her dirty bruised face.

"Don't say anything," she mouthed.

I shut up, wondering why she was warning me to keep quiet. *Is she so upset by my inability to help her, that she refuses to talk?*

Fly Guy made me strip (this time completely). Then he shackled me spread-eagled with back to the floor. The teenaged girl who, like me, was spread-eagled and shamefully exposed, turned her head away. Sadness gripped my heart as I saw myself through her eyes—nothing but a helpless helper.

Overwhelming weariness flooded me. My innards crying out for food, my throat parched, and my spirit spent, I fell into fitful sleep.

8. Excruciating Interrogation

8 a.m., Tuesday, April 3

The agony of being locked in an excruciating position kept me awake most of the night. If it weren't for the hope that only God can give, I would have surrendered to despair. I knew the girl must also be suffering, but for some reason, she wouldn't speak to me. This only added to my unrest.

Fly Guy came to loosen one hand so that we could eat the moldy doughnuts he brought and drink his coffee, 'freshly brewed.' It tasted like it should have been thrown out three years ago. But I drank it to assuage my intense thirst. I had barely finished his sumptuous feast when he launched into a barrage of questions, which I refused to answer.

"You idiot. You won't answer me." Fly Guy kicked me in the ribs. "Do you think Mac is going to be easier on you?" He opened his phone and punched in a number. "I've brought to you the would-be savior of our girl. He's dying to see you."

A chill went through me as Fly Guy emphasized the word 'dying.'

I looked across the attic to see Mac leaving one of the soundproof rooms. "That was delicious," he said as he closed the door. "I'll be back for more."

He walked across the creaky attic floor. Each step groaned under his weight. He looked at me with a smirk as he took off his belt. "You know how these interviews go?" he asked.

I wanted to say, "Yeah, I know. Your interrogations are bullying to the max. First, you tie your victim down, so he can't defend himself, then you torture him if his answers aren't as forthcoming as you'd like, then you try to frighten him with the promise of even worse torture if he doesn't give you the information you want."

That's what I wanted to say, but I decided to play the nice guy and appeal to his better self. "I'm thinking your interview will be humane." I flashed a generous smile. "So, let's get started."

I planned to weave a believable story that would lead them astray. My story included all the facts that I was sure they knew but added other details designed to mislead them.

As I answered Mac's questions, I maintained that the girl was my property. Recapturing her was my only reason for invading Mac's domain. I hinted that I had contacts who could make it very unpleasant for Mac if he continued to hold me and the girl against our will.

"So, you followed my man, Stanley, to find my primary location with the hopes of finding my girl? That's all?" Mac strutted back and forth between the girl and me, hands on his ample hips and his eyes fixed on the girl's body.

"Let's say I also wanted to get to know you better," I replied. "Our first meeting was much too short. Who knows? Maybe if we spent more time together, we could see how we could help each other."

"Sarcasm gets you nowhere with me." Mac stood with all his weight on my stretched-out thighs, sending excruciating pain upwards to the groin, downwards to the heels.

"What makes you think that I'm being sarcastic?" I asked, twisting, and gasping under the extreme pressure of his weight, I could hardly get five words out between gasps. "I can see ways we could be... of mutual benefit."

"I can't see where you could help me," Mac yawned loudly. "And I sure as hell ain't gonna help you."

"Take this girl, for instance....." I said. "I have a whole network of women... who can teach her... the finer things... of female arts... Things you gentlemen... can never teach." I couldn't read the girl's face because she had turned her head away from me, but there was no mistaking what she was saying with her middle finger. I continued. "It depends... on whether you want... a sophisticated call girl... who rakes in... five hundred or more... per client... or just a streetwalker... who nets... fifty to a hundred... per client. Just think about it.... You don't have to... decide now."

Mac stepped down off my thighs, which gave a measure of relief, but waves of throbbing pain still caught my breath. Even more painful was my anxiety over the effect of my proposal to make our girl into a sophisticated call girl. *Will she see it as my using her or as the ruse that it is?*

Without a word, Mac turned and went down the stairs with Fly Guy following close behind.

9. Focus on Her Eyes

10 a.m. Tuesday, April 3

I was furious, frustrated, and frightened.

Furious because of the cold-hearted cruelty these men were inflicting on an innocent girl.

Frustrated because my attempts to save her were making matters worse.

Frightened because this evil was spreading, infecting even fire fighters, who were the least likely to be corrupted, or so I thought. *Maybe the rumors of fire fighters deliberately delaying their response to fires at the businesses of the mayor's competitors are true. Who, then, can I trust?*

"I see now what you're up to." The girl broke into our silent reverie. "I've discussed for hours with my guidance counselor the thinking of writers like Tolstoy and C.S. Lewis. So, I know that devourers can disguise themselves as deliverers. Who knows? You could be wearing a mask of kindness to win me away from Mac so you can use me for your own dirty business."

"Wow, I'm impressed. What motivated you to read such deep-thinking authors?" I asked.

"When life hands you difficult questions the self-help crap that most people swallow doesn't cut it. My questions drive me to dig deeper and wider for answers that make sense."

"Was it because you saw the deceitful approach I employed on Mac, that you concluded that I was lying to you, too?" I asked.

"Isn't that logical?"

"Highly logical, but not necessarily true," I answered. "Actually, I was trying to convince Mac that I wasn't on the side of the law, so that he wouldn't see me as a threat. But as you saw, it didn't work. Still, the fact is, I do want to set you free."

"What you want has no chance of happening, so stop raising false hopes. Just shut up, 'cause I'm not listening," she snapped, releasing a heavy sigh.

"Just consider what I have to say."

"Talk all you want. What good will it do? Sure, the Bible and other holy books and most of our country's laws are on our side. But what good are the Bible's promises and man's laws when our fate is in the hands of men who couldn't care less about such things?"

"You're right. It looks hopeless. But until we take our last breath, the God who set Daniel free from the lions' den can rescue us," I said.

"Oh? How do you suppose he's gonna do that?"

"Two possible ways—Mac's superstition and the Mafia," I said.

"Now, I've heard everything," the girl let loose with a huge groan.

"No, you haven't heard everything," I responded. "I know people high up in the West Wend Mafia," I said. "I'll tell Mac and Fly Guy that my Mafia friends have found out how Mac has mistreated you, and they're furious. Because no one messes with the Mafia or their friends."

"How are your Mafia 'friends' supposed to find out, if we're the only ones who know and we're locked up?" the girl asked with a sarcastic tone.

"That's where you come in. Your job will be to convince them that after I set you free and before you were recaptured, you called your girlfriend whose dad is in the Mafia to ask for help. My job is to convince Mac and Stanley that you're telling the truth, and that your girlfriend's dad is a Mafia bigshot. Who knows if Mac will believe us? But even if all it does is make him second guess, he'll think twice before hurting you. If we're lucky, he'll set you free and try his best to disappear somewhere far from here."

"Set me free, you say? I'm never going to be free from the memory and pain of those two men... doing... what they did to me. And if they let me go from here, where to?" the girl asked.

"You can go to my home where you can have all the time you need to get back to normal."

"There is no getting back to normal after what I've been through," she said.

"That's true. Mac and Fly Guy have inflicted wounds that create life-long scars," I said. "But you can choose what the scars mean. You can let them make you bitter or better."

"Bitter. I get that. But how any of this can make anyone better is beyond me."

"You're right. It *is* beyond you. Beyond me. Beyond anyone. You have to reach beyond yourself, beyond this world, beyond the farthest star in the farthest galaxy. When you reach the Maker of all, who is beyond all he has made, you'll find him closer than your next breath. He's there to give you the wisdom that makes you better, not despite, but because of suffering horrible evil."

"No sermons, please. I'm too angry to even imagine that good can come out of this kind of evil."

"I'm sorry, I know better than to preach at someone feeling the kind of pain you've suffered. I should be listening."

"*You* should be listening? How about the one whom you say is beyond all, who made all, if there is such a person? I wish he would listen. I used to believe in him. Now I don't see how I can," the girl said. "I'd like to tell him a thing or two. I'd scream in his face, 'You failed! Failed! Failed! The world you made is a mess. If this is what you wanted, you fail to get my vote. And if you didn't want it this way, what's wrong with you? Why are you letting all this shit happen?'"

"You're right," I said. "God's world isn't the way he wants it. His grand scheme for people to explore, discover, and wisely govern the Earth has failed miserably."

As if to illustrate the point, a man burst out of one of the kinky rooms leveling virulent curses at the girl and leaving her sobbing. The man had the physique of a prize-winning bodybuilder. At my distance, it looked like blood was oozing from his massive neck. *Has he been bitten? Is this sadomasochism up close?* A stream of venomous obscenities poured from his mouth as he pulled his shirt over his well-sculpted torso. "You deserve the beating I gave you. You slimy whore. I'm not paying for this kind of sickening shit. I shoulda strangled...."

The uproar of his trail of vitriol diminished as he went down the stairs. Only then could I concentrate on the agonizing sobs coming from the room he had vacated. Heart-stabbing, haunting groans, punctuated by a retching cough and still more wracking sobs. Sobs that spilled from the abused woman's soul into my soul and spread to the girl beside me. Helpless in my effort to keep back the tears, I surrendered to grief.

"Lord, have mercy on that wounded woman," I whispered.

The girl turned to me, looking into my tear-filled eyes, and said, "You do care."

"Yes, I care."

"But what good is your caring?" the girl said. "We're trapped. They will dispose of you and make me a sex slave. I can see it coming. There's nothing we can do about it."

"There's only one thing that can keep us from caving in...." I paused, realizing I didn't know her name. "But first, we should know each other's name." I smiled and bowed slightly. "Ladies first."

"I'm Heather. Heather Osborne."

"And I'm Dave. Dave Von Moeller."

"Well, Ms. Osborne, the key to winning any battle is Hope. Lose hope and you've lost the fight. And the only hope we have of getting out of this alive is if God himself delivers us."

"Oh, so we just lay here and let God swoop down and rescue us, right?" Her voice conveyed her disbelief.

"No, we work together with God which means we'll have to trust each other and him. Can you lay aside your fear, anger, and distrust?

"Well, I don't know if I can ever forgive you for telling Mac you could arrange to make me into a sophisticated call girl." Heather stuck out her lower lip, displaying exaggerated pouting.

Is she just trying to rub it in? But her lips curled into a slight smile to show she was teasing me. "You remind me of my daughter, Jenna, who turned sixteen today. She's always making fun of me."

"I'm the same age," Heather said.

Anger flooded my chest as I thought of 16-year-olds violated as Heather had been. "I want to do for you what I hope someone would do for Jenna if she were trapped like you are, Heather. I would want them to get her safely back to her family."

"But I don't have a family to go back to."

"Does that mean there's no one you can trust in your family?"

"It's okay when it's just me and my mom and sister, but when Hank, my stepdad, is home, he's always tormenting me. And my mom does nothing to stop it."

"So, she leaves you to deal with your mean stepdad all by yourself?"

"Yeah. And you're right to call him 'mean.'" Heather winced as she pulled against the ropes that held her. "Just because I stayed out late one night with my boyfriend, Hank calls me a whore."

"That's not merely mean. That's cruel!"

"You should hear the things he says to my mom. He's vicious. He never notices the good things she does— cleaning the house, doing the laundry, washing the dishes. The more she beautifies the house and yard, the more he accuses her of trying to attract lovers. Then he beats her."

"Has he ever beaten you?"

"Not really, except with words. He calls me lazy, stupid, mentally deranged, and wasteful. Not once has he said 'thank you' to mom or me. We exist under the cloud of his permanent scowl."

"I can see how that could be unbearable, but running away to the red-light district?" I asked.

"I got in an argument with Hank that ended with my saying that I'd be better off living on the streets than taking his abuse. That infuriated him. I could tell he was raging because the skin on his neck turned purple. He grabbed me, threw me in the car, and brought me to this part of town. Then he yanked me out, dumped me on the sidewalk, and said, 'So you wanna live with tramps? See what it's like to live with sluts like yourself.'"

"Hmm, so you didn't choose to be here. Your stepdad forced you to fend for yourself in the most dangerous part of the city."

"Right. That first night, I slept on a couch that was on a ledge beneath the expressway. Three women and a man had couches up there. The man loaned me his couch while he slept on an old recliner. I should have stayed with those people, but I took off the next morning."

"Where did you go?" I asked.

"I just started walking toward home, looking for food on the way. I was checking out a trash bin behind a restaurant when I met Stanley and Mac. They asked if I'd like a good meal. I said, 'Of course.' We went to their place. They fed me. They must have spiked the food or drink with drugs because I felt so good. I would have done anything to feel that way again. I fell asleep. When I woke, I overheard them talking about what a good sex slave I would be. You know the rest of the story. You saw how they tied me up in the basement."

The door of one of the kinky rooms squeaked open. Framed in the doorway stood the mayor of West Wend. *No wonder West Wend is called 'Sin City.' Look at its leadership.* Heather and I witnessed the top official of our city zipping up his pants as he hurriedly left a room devoted to sexual deviance.

"Talk about wild sex...." Mayor Russell T. Molson was talking on his phone. "You've got to do it with Krystyl. Her body is super erotic. I'd tell you more but I'm late for a Council meeting."

"Oh God, protect that woman from such evil men," I prayed. "And bring swift and devastating judgment on the mayor for his cruel, cold-hearted treatment of her. Give us leaders who honor women...."

"Do you mean what you just prayed?" Heather asked me.

"It's what God wants... that men should honor women, not disgrace them," I said.

The mayor's exit left us aghast. My heart pounded so angrily it took my breath away. Heather turned pale.

"He talked as if it were just a thrill, like a ride on the Midway." Heather began to shake.

"Not the kind of behavior you expect from a city leader, is it? What these men do to women, the lust in their eyes as they look at women makes my blood boil," I said.

"You don't know the half of it," Heather responded. "My stepdad did it to my mom. My boyfriend did it to me... They treat you like toys to be played with, then discarded."

"And that makes you feel...?" I asked.

A long silence allowed feelings to bubble to the surface. She described those feelings in words like 'helpless, hopeless, angry, mad, afraid, dirty, trapped, unloved, filthy, foul...'

Gently, I said, "A true man stays with his wife to protect and support her. True men fight to keep the world safe for their wives and daughters. The men in your life did the opposite— they abused and abandoned you, leaving you to fight alone for yourself. And because the most important men that you know have cruelly treated you, you must find it hard to trust any man."

"It's true. In my world, men are sly wolves to avoid or fight off... All men, even Mayor Molson... All men, except for...."

"Except for?" I prodded.

"Except for you."

"I thought you might say that, Heather. The sad fact is, I am just like all the rest, except that Jesus came into my life and showed me how men should treat women. It's his Spirit that walks beside me and gives me the desire and power to treat women with respect. My point is, it's not mainly me who makes you feel safe. It's Jesus. He lives in me. And he respects you and genuinely loves you. And he makes that love known to you through me."

"Is that why I feel like you don't have your eyes on me in the way that most men look at me? You know... like the way Mac and Fly Guy look at me as if they want to jump on me."

"To tell the truth, I've been tempted to look on you with lust. But Jesus has helped me focus on your face, not your body.

"The face provides a window to the soul, especially the eyes. So, when I see you, I focus on your eyes. They tell me when you are afraid... relieved... sad... angry...happy...."

"I wondered how you were dealing with my being naked," Heather said.

"If I had focused on your body, I wouldn't have come to know you. But I think I know you, the real you, to some extent, because I've focused on what your face has told me through your eyes and your voice."

"I appreciate how you avoid looking at my body."

10. What Women Should Know About Men

"Women struggle with lust too," Heather said. "But what you describe seems more constant. It's like you have a demon ready at the slightest provocation to ignite flames of lust."

"That's pretty accurate, Heather."

"If that's the case, how do you deal with it? And how can women help men with this?"

"Since your father is not likely to talk with you about this, I'll tell you what I think fathers should tell their daughters," I said.

She nodded.

"We've already said that men are easily turned on, sexually. Women can help them by dressing modestly and by not being intentionally suggestive in their words and body language. But God holds men responsible for their thoughts and behavior, even if women are immodest. So, a man is lying when he tells a woman, 'You made me do it. You're so sexy. I couldn't resist the urge to go all the way.' If I give in to such lustful thoughts, that's my fault."

"How do you stop thinking in a lustful way about women, especially immodest women?"

"I've built up around myself what I call my seven temptation blockers.

"One, be realistic. Does lusting for sex with any pretty woman I see, make sense? I keep reminding myself that I am old enough to be your father, that my daughter, Jenna, is your age.

"Two, do to others what you wish others would do to you. Would I want a man in this situation to keep his eyes off Jenna? You had better believe I would.

"Three, ask what would my wife and Jenna wish me to do?

"Four, I ask myself if I want all that comes with the few minutes of pleasure. Do I want the guilt of being unfaithful to my wife? Can I endure the shame I'll feel when she finds out what I did? With all she's done for me, do I wish to cause her to doubt my love and appreciation? After all, consorting with another woman suggests that I'm not satisfied with my wife. What is she to do with her rage because of my betrayal?

"Sometimes, I get rough with myself, saying: You filthy-minded beast, you dirty old man. How could you?

"Six, I agree with Jesus who says looking at a woman with lust in my heart is fornication. So, when tempted, I say to myself, 'What kind of pleasure do I want? The temporary pleasure of satisfying my sinful lusts? Or the long-lasting pleasure of pleasing Jesus and treating women respectfully?'

"But the major safeguard which keeps me thinking rightly and has kept me from lust in the situation we are now in, Heather, is imagining Jesus is here with us and then doing what he would do in this situation. He, like us, was stripped naked. You know the shame we feel. Think of the shame he felt while crowds of people stared at his naked body painfully stretched out on a Roman cross. You better believe he understands what we're going through. And what did he do while he was in a situation worse than ours? Although they mocked him, he did not mock his tormentors or complain about his fickle friends who abandoned him.

"He promised the repentant thief a place in paradise with him. He provided a family for his mother, Mary. He offered forgiveness to those who were rejecting him and torturing him. The point? He was lifting people up while they were putting him down.

"I want to be like Jesus. So, I choose to treat you with respect, the way Jesus treated women. I choose to love you as Jesus loves you. Jesus was pure in his treatment of people, so they felt safe around him. I want to be pure in my treatment of you so you can be sure you are safe with me."

"Wow, that's unreal," Heather said through her tears.

"If you catch me failing to be like Jesus in how I treat women, call me on it, please."

11. Mafia to Free Heather?

3 p.m. Tuesday, April 3

My scheme for escaping Mac's trap demanded daring bravado and cool steadiness. "We can outfox Mac," I assured Heather. "But only if God fills him with fear.

"Listen carefully. I've spent hours creating this story. It's crazy and somewhat unrealistic. Yet it might scare Mac since he seems to be superstitious. I've seen him rubbing a rabbit foot he keeps in his pocket. And he's got a four-leaf clover embedded in his necklace. He freaked out when a black cat snuck in the basement window that Stanley left open."

"So, we know he believes crazy stuff. Maybe he will believe my crazy story. It has enough truth in it about the West Wend Mafia to make it believable.

"So, here's the plan. First, we tell Mac that you, Heather, have been welcomed into the West Wend Mafia through your friend, Hope, the daughter of 'Davey the Doughnut' Aceto."

"Davey the Doughnut? You gotta be kidding...." Heather laughed.

"No joke. We have a file on him at the main precinct. Sometime, I'll tell you the story of how he got that nickname. But for now, all you need to know is that his daughter, Hope, is your friend, and through her you've been adopted into the Mafia. Mr. Aceto is high up in the organization. And he's furious since he found out through your phone call to Hope how Stanley and Mac have treated you, Heather."

"What if Mac contacts the Mafia to check out our story?" Heather asked.

"Some of my story is true. Besides, it's extremely hard to contact someone in the upper levels of the Mafia," I answered. "You have to go through the front-line underlings who ask trick questions and want to see if you know the passwords, which change often. I've kept informed about their movements since my early years as a cop, and now as a private investigator."

"I'm assuming Mac doesn't know the Mafia very well," I told Heather, "or he would not have started working in West Wend without agreeing to pay a percentage of his profits to the Mafia. However, Mac may know some Mafia names. So, I am ready to use them."

12. Mac and Fly Guy Flee

4 p.m. Tuesday, April 3

"I think there's more that you need to tell me before we finish things off," Mac stroked the barrel of his Glock 17.

"And I have more to tell you," I said. "In talking with Heather, I discovered she is friends with members of the West Wend Mafia, and it's dangerous for you to be holding her, let alone abusing her."

"What makes you so sure she belongs to the West Wend Mafia?" Mac asked. "Didn't you say she belongs to you?"

"Yes, I did. But she was just another girl that I bought from a pimp. I didn't know much about her until you gave me such a good opportunity to talk with her by placing us here together.

"Did you know that she has a girlfriend in a top Mafia family?" I paused to see if what I said registered with them. It seemed to go over their heads. "Since I learned that she calls 'Joe the Hood' her uncle, I have dropped all claims on Heather... You must know who 'Joe the Hood' is?"

Mac and Fly Guy looked at each other, shrugging. "Mafia?" Fly Guy ventured.

"Near the top!" I said. "He's a capo!" I looked at the two men, and as I feared, their faces were blank. "Capo is short for caporegime, the rank just beneath the Mafia underboss. 'Joe the

Hood' and Heather's friend's dad, 'Davey the Doughnut' Aceto, are West Wend Mafia caporegimes."

"Wait! Did you say, 'Davey the Doughnut'?" Stanley asked.

"Yep," I responded indifferently.

Mac and Stanley looked at each other and back at me, as I lay at their feet in utter vulnerability. It was as if I had told a joke with a long story and had finally come to the punch line. They both roared in laughter and began kicking me, almost in jest.

"I'm telling you the truth. This is only making it worse for you," I said.

"You gotta be crazy. Whoever heard of a Mafia capo named 'Doughnut'?"

"Everyone connected with the West Wend Mafia knows about the Doughnut," I shouted between kicks to the ribs.

I could see by their response how little they knew about the West Wend Mafia and the danger they faced by infringing on Mafia territory. Part of that territory was Heather, who decided it was time for her to enter the fracas and stake her claim.

With a heart-arresting scream, Heather commanded, "Stop! Stop kicking my friend. With each kick, you're only adding to your punishment from Uncle Joe and Mr. Aceto."

"Shut up, you slut or...."

"No, you shut up, Stanley," Mac said. "I gotta think... If Dave and Heather's story is true, we're in big trouble. And the fact that he used the name 'Doughnut' makes the story more believable, not less. What liar would make up such a crazy name for a Mafia big shot? Even if they are lying, the fact is our business is irritating the Mafia... That means you and I have only one option—disappear."

"Before you vanish could you set us free?" I asked.

"What? And have you cause more trouble before we have a chance to leave? No way," Mac said. "Be grateful we left you alive."

"Why not finish them off?" Stanley proposed.

"Idiot! If they're telling the truth, that would guarantee the Mafia would hunt us down," Mac said.

"But they could be witnesses against us," said Stanley, his voice trailing as they descended from the attic.

Mac put in the last word: "Which would you rather face, a jury or the Mafia?"

13. All But One Saved from the Fire

5 p.m., Tuesday, April 3

I assumed Mac and his sidekick, Stanley aka Fly Guy, did not want anyone noticing they were leaving— permanently. If at any moment the Mafia was returning to reclaim the territory Mac and Fly Guy had usurped, Mac and his partner would want their disappearance to be sudden and shrouded in secrecy. That's why they failed to shackle my right hand with a cuff. They used rope instead because they couldn't find another cuff.

I imagined them slipping silently away.

"Now what?" Heather broke into my thoughts.

"We get out of here," I said.

"As if we could move," Heather said sarcastically. "And think of the fashion statement we'd make, dressed as we are. Or shall I say undressed?" Heather snickered.

"Glad to see your humor lurking beneath the surface. We'll probably need a lot of it before this is over."

"Can't promise," Heather said, "but I'll try to pay attention to the bright side."

"Speaking of bright side, my ropes are the flimsy laundry-type ropes. Maybe I can rub through them." I began rubbing the rope around my wrist on the rough floor.

"Meanwhile, the show seems to be going on, even though the producers have fled," I said, as I kept rubbing the rope. "Must be Mac didn't even tell the Madam they were leaving, so she's left running the place."

"She's got a lot of traffic down on the second and first floors. I can hear people shuffling around down there all the time," Heather said. "And clients are still coming up here to the kinky rooms. But it's no use crying out to them for help. None of them wants to be seen in a place like this, so they won't slow down to consider our pleas as they sneak out."

"Do you smell smoke?" Heather asked.

"No... On second sniff, yes!" I answered. "I bet Mac and Fly Guy set a fire to destroy evidence of what they were doing here."

"And to kill witnesses like us," Heather said, "if we don't somehow escape these shackles."

The whole building erupted in screams. 'F-bombs' exploded in every direction. We hollered for help, but no one paid attention to us. Attendants escorted screaming clients in various stages of undress from the kinky rooms, but none of the so-called prostitutes came out. Why? I heard women crying, "Don't leave us here!"

So far, we could see no flames or smoke, but we could smell the smoke. *How much time before we are fried meat?* I wondered. The floor was getting warmer. *Who knows when the floor would burst into flames?* I rubbed the rope even more furiously. "At last, it's frayed!" Desperate, I pulled at the rope with adrenaline-fueled strength. Snap! "My right hand is free!"

After rubbing for a seemingly unending minute, I had frayed the rope tying my left hand to the cuff. I pulled on it. It frayed a bit more but held. *The floor is getting hotter.* Again, I yanked, and the rope broke.

With two hands free, I turned to rubbing the ropes tied to the shackles that bound my two feet. The smoke filled the upper reaches of the attic roof, leaving those of us on the attic floor still able to breathe. A few more minutes of rubbing and yanking freed my feet. When I tried to stand, I buckled over, unable to bear the cramping pain caused by being tied rigidly for so long in the spread-eagle position. I crawled to the nearby closet where my captors had stuffed my clothes. Tongues of flame were beginning to lick the cracks in the floorboards.

From the lining in my pants, I took a slender knife and cut Heather free. She grabbed her clothes from the same closet. Then I pointed her to the kinky rooms, and beyond, to the door on the far wall. "I don't see any flames yet in that half of the building. Go there and get dressed. Then see where the door on the far wall leads. I hope it's a fire escape. After I finish dressing, I'll be trying to set the people free in the small rooms," I said.

#

I'd love to forget what I saw in the first room. Remember the room from which we heard such heart-crushing sobs? I now saw the source of that weeping. She sat on a mattress in a yoga meditation position, hands on her knees, palms up, staring into nothingness. Blood dribbled from her mouth. Her right eye was swollen shut. Her heavy naked body displayed deep scratches. I covered her with a blanket from the corner of her room, cut the rope that tied her to the wall, and urged her to flee the fire. She just sat there. *Is she in a trance?*

"Come. We've gotten go," I urged. But she was on another planet. I took her hand and tugged. She screamed, swiping at my face with her long, sharpened fingernails.

"Let me go to hell where I belong." She kept babbling, "Hell! Where I belong!"

"No!" I grabbed her by the wrists so she couldn't slice me with her nails. "You belong in a place of safety, peace, love, and lasting joy. Come with...." With superhuman strength, she yanked herself out of my grasp, sneered at me, and ran toward the side of the attic where flames had broken through the floor. As she approached the far wall, flames leapt to her long hair, she slowed her pace and walked, as if in a wedding march. Then she stood, surrounded by the highest flames.

How can she still be standing? I stood transfixed as the floorboards crumbled beneath her weight and she fell into the holocaust below, screaming, "It's not over! It has just begun."

Slap! Slap! "It's Heather, Dave. We've got to hurry," she screamed as she pulled me back to our current crisis. There was no time to process the horror I had witnessed. It became a permanent scar on my memory.

Heather's tug on my arm made me sense the urgency of our task. "By the way, the door you sent me to check out is a fire escape."

"Thank God," I shouted.

"How 'bout thanking me?" Heather stuck out her lower lip but couldn't suppress a smile.

In the second room, a woman of striking ebony hue both begged and commanded, "Don't let them burn me alive!"

"We won't," I assured her. In the corner, out of her reach, lay a blanket and her crumpled clothes. Heather threw the blanket around her while I attended to her shackles. Screwed into the floor beside the mattress was an eyebolt to which was attached a synthetic soft shackle rope with a protective sleeve around her right ankle. *Concern for ankle, but not for soul.*

As I sawed through the rope, I thanked God no one had found and confiscated my slender, razor-sharp stiletto. I thanked him also for my wife, Kate, who had sewed a pocket for the knife on the inside of the leg of my pants. *When am I going to see Kate? How about the girl I'm setting free here? Does this woman have a home to go to?*

I asked her and she replied, "I'm not sure."

"We are Dave and Heather. I'll let you figure out who's who... And don't mind my joking around," I said. "It's my way of dealing with stress."

"I'm Ana... spelled with one 'n'."

As I freed Ana's leg, I asked Heather to go to the next room to cover the occupant with a blanket and tell her I was coming.

I handed Ana her crumpled clothes so she could dress. "Bring your blanket with you."

Meanwhile, in the next cubicle, Heather found a woman with red, shoulder-length hair. She was hammering away on her shackle rope with a sharp-edged flint rock that she said had fallen out of one of her customer's pockets. The rope was already frayed, so I was able to quickly cut through the rest of it. "Excellent work, young woman," I said. "You saved us some time. Bring your blanket and come with us."

I noticed that the flames on the other side of the attic were coming our way. Hurriedly, I opened the door to the last cubicle. The occupant looked like a Southeast Asian woman with bobbed black hair. She put her hands up in front of her face, trying to fend me off. "It's too late to save me. Just go!"

"We don't have time for heroics. We need you with us," I said, making quick work of slicing through the rope holding her leg.

We were all clothed and headed for the door to the fire escape when a boom from below knocked us to the floor.

I barked out orders. "Everyone stay down. Use a corner of your blanket for a facemask. Follow Heather to the door. Crawl. I'll bring up the rear."

Heather began coughing. She and I had no blanket for facemasks. *It's taking her forever to get to the door. Is she lost?*

"It's so smoky," Heather cried. "I can't find the door."

"Go the way the floorboards are laid," I directed. "That way you'll find the wall, then the door." I was coughing so much, I wondered if Heather understood me. Assuming she might have passed out, I was about to call the others to follow me when Heather shouted,

"I found it."

Along with the smoke billowing from the door, the five of us, smeared with soot and seared by heat, tumbled out. We flopped like rag dolls on the landing and top stairs of the fire escape. "We can't stay in this building ," I warned, "I have a premonition, a feeling, it's going to explode."

Somehow, each of us gathered the strength to stand and climb down the stairs, holding onto the rail. I couldn't believe it. *Was it God or adrenaline? Or both! After all, who gave us adrenaline?*

Behind the mansion, weeds competed with overgrown shrubs beyond which a barely discernible path led into thick dark woods. I was leading the crew along the path when we felt a sudden whooshing boom that would have knocked us flat had we been near the mansion. As it was, some of us stumbled. "Keep going," I urged.

I helped Ana get to her feet, and then I turned to help the Southeast Asian woman, but she had already regained her footing and was well on the way into the woods. Heather and the red head supported each other as they tripped along.

Downed trees, broken limbs, thistles, and thorn bushes made our trek more like running the gauntlet than the pleasant walk I had hoped to find. About one hundred feet into the woods, we found a clearing with logs and stumps on which we could sit.

Before we sat, we enjoyed one of those unforgettable moments as we stood in a circle and looked at each other— hair singed, faces blackened by smoke and soot, bodies slumped by exhaustion, but all still alive. What else could we do but wonder and hug each other?

Each of us found a stump or log to sit on. We made introductions. I found out that the redhead's name was Marta and the Southeast Asian woman was Krystyl.

The woods were a mixture of walnut, oak, and pine. A stand of pine trees on the west side of the clearing had formed a soft bed from pine needles laid down over decades. On this bed, we all lay down. The women were soon fast asleep.

14. Carriage House Hideout

6 p.m., Tuesday, April 3

I was startled awake from nodding off by the chopping sound of a helicopter. *Oh no, they've discovered us.* My heart skipped a few beats, coming back in rhythm with a thud. *But wait, they would be circling overhead if they saw one of us sleeping here. Instead, the sound of that contraption is diminishing.* To keep us safe from discovery, especially from crooked police or nosy news reporters, I had made sure our people were sleeping beneath trees with lower branches that completely hid them.

After the helicopter scare, I decided to explore our surroundings. Fifteen minutes of stumbling and picking my way through and around brambles, fallen limbs, and uprooted trees, brought me to the front of what was probably the carriage house that went with the mansion. Its unusual distance from the mansion puzzled me. Originally built near the owner's larger home, carriage houses stored horse-drawn carriages and sometimes housed the coachman or caretaker on the upper floor. When automobiles replaced horses, many carriage houses were converted into small second homes. Several hundred feet stretched out between the mansion and the carriage house.

I didn't see the carriage house until I was twenty feet from it. That's how thick the woods had become. *Could there be a house in the city that is more secluded and difficult to reach?*

"I looked back at the riotous tangle I had just come through, and a smile played across my face. *Hmmm. This carriage house would be a good hideout until we find a more lasting place.*

The two-story building with vines covering its sides and the far-reaching branches of ancient maples forming a dome over it, blended into the woods. Vines had been cut away so that the unlocked door swung freely. I stepped inside to find a large open room with a kitchen and dining area on one side and a living room on the other. Sheets covered everything. Peeking under the sheets, I found two recliners, two couches, and a wooden table with ten chairs in the dining room. No electricity, but I found several camp lanterns that would supply adequate lighting. The oven and stove top burners worked, supplied by a propane tank stationed at the rear of the house.

#

"Wake up, ladies, we've found a place to stay," I said upon returning to the clearing where they slept. " Just think, we won't have to worry about rain or coyotes or rabid raccoons. No skunk snuggling up to you to share warmth.

"There's only one problem. We need to slash our way through brambles, fallen trees, and thick undergrowth to get to this house."

With reluctant sighs, the women gave up their soft pine-needle beds and headed with me to the carriage house. I admired their pluck as we tripped through the tangled underbrush. Each of us fell at least once, feet and legs dragging from soreness. The wildly strewn branches poked and scratched us continually. Nothing serious, only irritating.

At last, we stood inside the carriage house. Someone had covered the furniture with sheets. "Judging by the dust layered on the sheets, I'd guess no one's been here in the last ten years," I said. "Let's carefully take the sheets off, folding them inward so we capture the dust. Then we can shake the dust off outside.

While the others were removing the sheets, I fished around in the waste basket I found in the cupboard under the sink. "Voila!" I shouted. "Here's a receipt for a grocery item dated October 11, 2013. Today is 2018. That means someone was here about five years ago. So, we can safely assume not many people know about this house. The big question is, how long can we use this place to hide in, before being discovered?"

Krystyl ran around the whole circumference of the room. "It feels so good to be free!" She danced and laughed in such an infectious way that everyone else joined her, including me. And I never dance.

As I watched them jumping up and down and twirling around, I began to cry. *This is their first taste of freedom for God knows how long. They can't help but celebrate.*

After ten minutes of frolicking, they stopped and caught their breath.

Ana looked over at me, "Why are you crying?" Ana asked.

"I was stirred by the exuberance you showed as you celebrated being free at last," I said. "But now we need to do something to make sure you stay free. We need to find a place to hide in case the wrong people come looking for you."

Heather was already searching. "One of us could squeeze behind this refrigerator if it could be shoved out a bit.

Hmmm...The refrigerator has larger wheels than usual, which should make it easy to move out from the wall. But it won't budge," she said.

"Look for a lock release on each of the rear wheels," I said.

"I found the releases," Ana said. "Now let's see... Yes! Look how easily it moves out from the wall."

In the wall behind the refrigerator, a sliding panel covered an opening about five-feet high by two-feet wide. Ana set the panel aside, then stepped through the opening. "And here are steps leading down to... I can't see."

I grabbed a camp lantern, lit it, and handed it to Ana. "Use this." She leaned forward. "Check this out. It looks like a room is down there or a tunnel."

"I think I'll ask Ana to explore the room or tunnel with me," I said. "I'd like you, Heather, and Marta to find any food left in the cupboards, no matter how old it is. If its cans, and they aren't dented or bloated, they might be safe to eat. We'll just have to use our noses to make sure the food isn't spoiled. Krystyl, I'm sure you've noticed the drapes and curtains are pulled closed. Please make sure that not even the slightest opening is left to let snoopy people see inside. Although I don't expect visitors since we're surrounded by such thick woods, and the woods are cluttered with underbrush, as you well know."

"Now let's explore this place."

Ana squeezed through the opening behind the fridge and I followed. We stood on a landing where we found an oil lamp on a shelf. Behind the lamp, were old matchboxes filled with wooden matches. We lit the lamp, which illuminated a stairway going down to a tunnel with stone floors and walls. Oak beams held up the hardwood ceiling.

"People don't need to bend over to walk through this tunnel." Ana waved her hand in the space between the top of our heads and the ceiling. "It's got to be about seven-feet high and seven-feet wide."

Every twenty feet on both sides of the tunnel, we found a shelf in the wall holding a lamp that we lit. As we lit the fourth set of lamps, Ana and I could barely see the end of the tunnel.

"Where is this tunnel headed?" Ana asked.

"My hunch is this tunnel connects the carriage house to the mansion. The mansion looks like the homes built before the Civil War. If what I'm thinking is true, there are underground rooms alongside this tunnel where slaves hid on their escape route to freedom in Canada."

"I'm getting scared. What if this tunnel caves in on us?" Ana asked.

I knocked on one of the oak beams holding up the ceiling. "These beams are solid," I said. "No need to worry."

As we neared the far end of the tunnel, we could feel the heat of the smoldering mansion.

We hurried to tell the others what we had found and to hear their reports. Heather and Marta found food in the cupboards— cans of tuna, salmon, and chicken, baked beans, green beans, corn, coffee, and tea for us to test and hopefully eat. Krystyl assured us she had frustrated any potential peeping toms by leaving not even the slightest peephole around the closed drapes.

"Now, Ana, I'd like you to show the others what we found."

Ana led the other three through the hole in the wall to the bottom of the stairs where, because of the lamps, they could see down the long tunnel.

"This is scary," Krystyl said.

"That's for sure," Ana agreed.

"Why are you taking us through this long tunnel?" Marta protested.

"You need a safe place to hide while you decide exactly how you want to reenter the world," I said. "News reporters would like to use you to spice up and sensationalize their stories. The criminals who held you captive will be looking for a way to silence you because they fear what you could say about them.

"Remember how Ana's ancestors, Black slaves, escaped slavery through an Underground Railroad?" I asked. "That's what I hope this carriage house with its tunnel is for you women— a stop on the road to freedom. How long we stay here depends on how long it takes investigators to find out we escaped the fire. Meanwhile, this is a fairly good hideout."

"But do we have to stay down here?" Krystyl asked. "This tunnel freaks me out."

"No, we can go back up to the kitchen."

We passed from the tunnel to the kitchen, removed the sheet from the table, and sat around it. "The moment we hear anyone approaching the carriage house, dive for the tunnel," I said. "I'll be staying up here to deal with whoever is visiting. I'll slide the panel closed and push the refrigerator to the wall and lock the rear wheels.

"If you need to come back from the tunnel, slide the panel open and reach under the fridge to the back wheels to release the wheel locks. The refrigerator will easily push forward."

"How long will we be locked in here?" Ana asked.

"This house is locked from the inside," I said. "That means you can unlock it and leave at any time. Just be sure to tell one of us, so we can lock up after you. Before you leave, I hope you'll do whatever it takes to be ready for what you'll face out there."

"What do you think we'll face?" Krystyl asked.

"And how do we get ready for it?" Marta added.

"Each of you has to decide how she wants to talk about or tuck away your experiences and memories," I answered. "Some of you may want to move far from here and even establish a new identity to shake free from people who want to kill you or suck you back into slavery.

"So, what am I saying? This carriage house with its tunnel might give you a safe place to plan your next step. Pretty cool, huh?"

"Cool?" Heather asked, smiling. "We've come through one hell of a fire to get cool."

I gave Heather a fist bump. "That's exactly what is going to get us through this. Trust in God and a sense of humor."

15. Who Can I Trust?

10 p.m., Tuesday, April 3

Krystyl's brow wrinkled.

"Something troubling you?" I inquired.

"Where was the Fire Department?" Krystyl asked. "The fire station is only a few blocks away from the mansion. I didn't hear a siren until we were in the woods. That was at least fifteen minutes from the time the fire started."

"Krystyl, you've shown us two more things that we will need to do," I said. "One, pay attention to anything unusual. Two, be careful whom you trust. I don't care if he's a fire fighter, a police officer, or a popular preacher. If he misses appointments and makes flimsy excuses, don't depend on him to keep promises."

"But if you can't trust preachers, who can you trust?" Heather asked.

"Of all people, we expect preachers to be trustworthy, but should we automatically trust a person because he's a preacher? or a cop? or a fire fighter?"

"I trusted firefighters and they, together with the cops, turned me over to be a sex slave for Mac and Stanley," Heather said.

"So, don't trust preachers, cops, or firemen. Is that the lesson?" I asked.

"No. Of course not." Marta said. "The lesson is...we won't trust a firefighter or cop or preacher automatically—just because he's a cop or fireman or preacher."

"Exactly," Ana said.

"Okay, so what are the signs of a person you shouldn't trust?" Krystyl asked.

"Don't trust a sweet talker who tells you how beautiful, sexy, and shapely you are," Ana said. "I was under the influence of a man who attracted me with his sweet words. I can't believe how gullible I was. Never had anyone take an interest in me. I so desperately wanted to hear that I was beautiful, and he gave me what I wanted. He could have authored a book titled *A Thousand Ways to Tell a Woman She's Beautiful*. With his smooth words, he could get me to do anything, including stuff I now regret."

"One of my boyfriends started that way," Marta said. "Then once he got me hooked on drugs, he belittled me. He could have authored the book titled *A Thousand Ways to Tell a Woman She's Ugly*. When he wanted sex or money, he was so sweet. But the rest of the time he was bitter as sugarless chocolate."

"Here's another trustbuster," Krystyl added. "Don't trust a big spender. Robert showered me with expensive gifts—a gold necklace, a large flatscreen TV, Victoria's Secret negligée, and the latest iPhone. I thought I'd landed a millionaire. Then he started asking me for small favors— ten dollars here, fifty dollars there, two hundred for car repair, just until payday. I thought he was rich. He could pay it back easily, so why not loan him the money? Guess what I found out? All the gifts he gave me were hot items that he had stolen. He didn't even have a job."

"I once had a man who actually was rich," Marta said. "But the more he gave me, the more he demanded. He acted as if he owned me."

"We also need to avoid fake listeners. When I met Quinn, I loved that he listened," Ana said. "He was so tender. When my younger brother was killed by a rival gang, Quinn was the only one to ask how *I* was feeling. When I shared how shattered I was when my uncle sexually abused me, Quinn cried and promised, 'I'll care for you, protect you, and always love you.' Then he gave me a drug that he said would ease my pain. It not only made me forget my pain, but it also flooded me with pleasure. To shorten a long story, he got me hooked on drugs. That was his way of caring for me."

"I can see you all have a good handle on the kind of men to watch out for," I said. "This is a heavy subject. Are you sure you want to stay on it?"

"Talking doesn't tire me... Or me ...Or me... Or me," said Marta and the others. "As long as we are on an important topic. And what could be more important than learning how to deal with the male half of humanity?"

"Food," Krystyl said. "Old Cambodian proverb say, 'Ideas lost if tummy empty.'"

Laughter erupted. Heather and Marta showed us the cupboards and we went to work on discovering what food was safe to eat as we clumsily tried to open the cans with an old rusty can opener.

While Marta and I tried to open all the cans, we sat around the table swapping stories and jokes. Small talk.

Heather suggested that we thank God for preserving our lives and for this food. We agreed, except for Krystyl who preferred to thank Mother Earth.

"Thank you, Lord, for preserving us so far, and please preserve us while we eat this very well-preserved food!" I quipped.

"While we are eating, let me tell you about another kind of person to be very careful to steer clear of," I said. "Never come under the influence of someone who tries to take you away from your support and keep you exclusively for himself. I have a friend whose husband treats her friends and relatives with such scorn that he has driven them away. He wants my friend to serve him and him alone. And he doesn't want anyone around to witness the punishment he lays on her if she doesn't serve him in the way he wants to be served."

"Damn, she ain't got no husband," Ana said. "She got herself a pimp."

"Thass fo sho," Krystyl agreed, trying to copy Ana's dialect.

"She needs to get away from that man before he controls her to death," Marta said.

Ana's dark curls sprang as she shook her head, rolled her dark eyes, and said, "Experience tells me men are deceptive predators."

"I've wondered if any man can be trusted." Marta said, with one eyebrow raised.

"You're joking," Heather said.

"Couldn't be more serious," Marta stood with her hands on her hips as she looked down her nose at the teenager. "Do you know any man that you can trust?"

"Sure," Heather said. "My guidance counselor has never let me down."

"Did you sleep with him? Live with him?" Marta asked. "Anyone can look good at work, but what's he like at home?"

"You think I'm just a naive kid." A flush of red flooded Heather's face as her hands hardened into fists. "I don't need an old hag like you...."

Krystyl interrupted Marta and Heather. "Let's say we wanted to create the ideal man," Krystyl said. "What would he be like?"

"He would be a man who listens, who looks me in the eyes, and encourages me... Like he really wants to know me and understand me," Ana said.

"I fantasize about having a man who would take me to recovery group or introduce me to other welcoming friends who encourage each other to do what's right, even if it's hard, very hard," Krystyl added.

"I'm tired of people who promise to get me out of my troubles when they can't handle life any better than I," Marta said. "They add to my troubles. I wish I had someone who is winning where I'm losing and who wants to help me learn how to win."

"I'm not sure I want to be that dependent on anyone, let alone my boyfriend," Ana said.

Krystyl began to rub her eyes. Marta yawned. Heather joined in the yawning. "Your yawns tell me we better see to sleeping arrangements soon," I interrupted. "We could bed down on these recliners and couches, but I'd be surprised if there weren't a room somewhere off to the side of the tunnel. So, let's explore the tunnel more thoroughly.

"We'll be looking for a removable panel that could lead us to a passageway to a room to hide slaves. I know some of you fear being in the tunnel. But which is safer, a tunnel that is secured by solid oak beams and is well-hidden or this above-ground part of the carriage house where you are sure to be caught if wrong people come here."

"Again, what makes you think there is a room down there?" Ana asked.

"I spent a day locked up with a firefighter who knew a lot about the Underground Railroad. This carriage house with its tunnel to the mansion fits the description he gave me of the hidden housing rich abolitionists provided for runaway slaves. Rooms were on either side of the tunnel. That's what we're looking for."

After a half hour of searching, Heather shouted, "I found a passageway."

The passageway, lined with hardwood, allowed only one person through at a time. "It leads to a room," Heather said, as she opened a door at the end of the passageway.

I wonder how many slaves hoping for freedom came through this passageway to their sleeping quarters. I brought up the rear, so by the time I entered the room, the lamps of the others showed that we had gained access to a dark, dusty room. "Well, I guessed right about sleeping quarters being here," I said.

We found two bunk beds built into the wall and three stand-alone cots.

"Pick your bed," I said. "Take these old blankets, and go shake them in the hallway, so you won't be breathing in so much dust while you sleep."

"We are so dirty, that I don't think it matters, but okay," Ana said.

I looked at the weary, soot-stained girls, "Sleep as best you can."

"What about you?" Ana asked.

"I'm sleeping in the living room," I said.

Krystyl came up to me and ran her fingers softly down my arm. "Why not with us?" Krystyl sounded seductive. "We could give you the ultimate massage and send you off to the sweetest sleep you've ever had. You deserve it after all you've done for us."

She's offering sex as if it were a normal way to say, 'thank you.' My brain froze. Animal instinct usurped my will. Torrents of desire smashed all my taboos. I would have yielded like a dog in heat if it weren't for that 'how could you?' look Heather gave me. That piercing glare unlocked my brain. I could think again. I could question—*what am I, man, or beast?* I could remember how demeaning and enslaving it was to be controlled by sex and how uplifting and freeing it was to have Christ in control of my passions. I was free—to be what I was created to be. I was free to be faithful to my wife and to show these women the goodness of faithfulness. So, I ignored Krystyl's offer.

"I want to keep any intruders from coming any closer to you than the kitchen," I explained. I, again, wished them a good night's sleep and exited.

I barely got away when I heard someone following me. "I have some questions for you," Heather said.

"I hope I can answer them." We went into the tunnel, illumined by the lamps Ana and I had lit earlier, and sat with our backs against the wall.

"First, what were you thinking when Krystyl propositioned you?" Heather asked. "It looked like you were eager to accept."

I wanted to defend myself, to protect my image, to act as if I were impervious to sexual attractions, but I knew Heather would see through such pretense, so I decided to be real. "You're right. Krystyl's invitation tempted me."

"But how could you feel that way toward Krystyl? She's your friend. Do you use your friends that way? If so, how could you?"

"I wasn't thinking. If I had been thinking, I would have told myself that this girl may not realize how demeaning it is to use sex as a payment—demeaning to herself and me. I can now show her the 'more excellent way.'"

"More excellent way?" Heather was shaking, her voice trembling. "What high and mighty nonsense are you talking about? How are you, if you're so weak, going to show Krystyl or anyone anything good?"

I sat in stunned silence, trying to speak, but unable to form the words. So, Heather continued.

"Remember when we were stripped naked and bound?" Heather asked. "You said you were tempted to look and lust. And now I find out you almost gave in to Krystyl's proposition. What's with you guys? Are you all that weak? I thought I could look up to you. Like you were the dad I always wanted. But, no, you're just like all the rest."

"You're right," I admitted. "I wouldn't be surprised if most men are as weak as I am when it comes to sex. I know for sure that if I am not depending on strength given to me by the Lord Jesus, I am likely, if tempted, to indulge my lustful cravings."

"So, women should stay away from men because they're all lusting...."

"No, I think, if a man is friends with a woman, he is far less likely to sexually fantasize about her. As you said, Heather, how could I take advantage of a friend like Krystyl?"

"But it's impossible to befriend every man so that they're all thinking rightly of me."

"I wish all women wanted men to think rightly of them, as you say. But what goes on in a man's mind is not your responsibility. God holds men responsible for their thoughts. Of course, women can help by being modest. But even if a woman is seductive, a man is responsible for how he thinks.

For example, I was responsible for what I thought of Krystyl's proposition, and when I looked at you, Heather, your face was saying 'how could you?' That look on your face broke the spell I was under, thawed my mind, and freed me to treat Krystyl the way Jesus would treat her. Thank you for helping me."

"So, let me get this straight." Heather circled her head with her delicate hands as if trying to prevent it from bursting as she stretched her mind around the idea. "You're saying men get turned on in a flash, even good men. So, they need Jesus' help to think rightly and act purely toward women?"

"That's not what I said, but it's what I meant. It's not that men are constantly fantasizing," I said. "If we've given our lives to Jesus, we see how he treated women and do likewise. Women were safe around Jesus. He never used them to satisfy his selfish desires. His love for them was pure. Loving people purely is the 'more excellent way' I mentioned earlier... and one more thing before you rejoin the other women."

"Why do I feel like you're about to hit me with another sermon?" Heather asked.

"Is that how you feel about my gems of wisdom?" I joked.

"No, I love hearing your wise sayings. It's as if you're the dad I always needed," Heather said. "So, preach it, Daddy-o."

"I've noticed how well you remember and practice what I teach you. I want you to know how happy that makes me."

"Yes, I remember good things you taught me," Heather said. "I treasure them." Heather looked down at her clenched fists. She paused. I noticed her cheeks reddening. "But I have an awful lot to forget that my stepdad has drilled into me. I hate him, not only for what he has done to my mother and me but for the memories of it that keep coming back to torture me."

"I want to know what that's been like for you, Heather, when we're not so sleep-deprived. Meanwhile, the last thing I wanted to tell you was to keep in mind that God is making something good out of the worst evils your stepfather inflicted on you. For example, your stepfather abandoned you to fend for yourself in the worst part of the city— that was cruel. But good came from it. In one of the most wretched places in the world, you've come face-to-face with your heavenly Father."

With that, I nodded toward the passageway. She took the hint and joined the girls while I went back through the tunnel to find a couch to sleep on.

16. Dawn Visitors

5 a.m. Wednesday, April 4

I woke from a deep sleep at dawn. Someone was tapping on the door. Having slept in my clothes, I was ready to either flee to the tunnel or answer the door. I pulled back a window cover, ever so slightly, and peeked at my visitors.

Could it be? That bald guy looks like Ron, (the firefighter, who endured the better part of a day with me in the stuffy hideout box at the police community center). The other guy was Al (the cop in charge of the center). I threw open the door.

If it weren't for Ron's finger pressed against his lips, I would have shouted my pleasure at seeing these friends. As it was, I quietly welcomed them and locked the door behind them.

"How did you find me?" I asked.

"With great difficulty, we've been looking all over for you." Ron said. "Because of the suspicious nature of the fire, we wondered if you might have been an intended victim of it. We got a lead when a firefighter reported that he thought he saw someone running from the mansion to the woods behind the mansion. The smoke was so thick he couldn't be sure. We were hoping it was you. We stumbled upon this house, after searching all night."

"So how many other people know about this place?" I queried.

" I told my partner, Joe," Al said.

"And I told my lifetime fire-fighting buddy, Pete, the whole story since I trust Pete. He's been letting us know which firefighters would be on our side," Ron said.

"Pete told those firefighters to call him if they saw anything that could lead us to you. That's how we got the calls giving us the lead to check this area."

"Hope we check out fine," I said.

"You said 'we.'" Al's face bore a question mark. "Are there others? Did Heather get rescued?"

"Yes, and more, but let's move to the kitchen before we talk about them."

Rummaging around in the cupboard, I found a saucepan which I filled with water and put on the stove for instant coffee. "Now, I want to know how my family is doing."

"They'll be pleased to know you are okay. They wanted you to know they are praying for you and for whoever you are helping." Al said.

"You can tell them we are helping three women forced into prostitution, and one teenaged girl being coerced by torture to learn the trade. When I found them, all four were stripped naked and tied by rope, obviously unwilling slaves. It was a struggle to free them before the mansion burned down."

Ron sucked in a huge breath, then slowly released it.

"Yeah, it knocked the wind out of me, too," I said. "We're talking slavery! These women were not there of their own free will just earning a bit more money for themselves and their families. They were lining the pockets of their owners who paid them barely enough food to survive."

"We've got to help them," Al said. "What would be a safe place for these women? How do we get them there? Who can best help them recover from what they've gone through?"

"I'd love for Heather to be sister to my daughter, Jenna," I said. "They would be good for each other. But I can't do that until I know it's safe for me to go home."

"At this point, we can't say for sure," Al said. "Nobody knows who you are, they are just looking for someone of your description."

"Okay, but here's what I'd most like to know," I said, "how to scare off this city's corrupt leadership. I've seen police and firemen protecting the sex-trafficking business and the mayor enjoying the kinky sex it offers. We don't know how widespread this is. But I want to get a clearer picture of human trafficking in our city and create a plan to expose and eliminate it."

Al inserted a low whistle. "That's a dangerous mission," he said. "People make big bucks off this business. They aren't going to give that up without a fight."

"That's why the battle needs to be carefully planned," Ron said. "We've talked to a lot of the older firefighters. Some say the corruption is too widespread to root out. Others want the people to know what's going on."

"I wonder if the fire chief, police chief and the mayor were involved in letting that mansion burn to the ground. If they were, then they are guilty of burning one person alive," I mused. "She preferred death over living with what they had done to her. And more would have perished if Heather and I had not been there to help them escape."

"And after all that's already been done for them, they will still perish if we don't find the right way to keep them from those men," Al said. "Hopefully, the authorities think the fire killed you all. That will give us more time to figure out what to do."

"It's obviously too risky to turn them over to the police," I said, as I served the coffee. "Besides, we don't know where two of the principal culprits, Mac and Stanley, are hiding. They could be on their way to Costa Rica or Australia or even Albania. So why try to hunt them down?" Al asked.

"Especially when corrupt members of the police force would lie under oath, making it difficult to get a conviction," Ron added. "But worst of all, it would require these women with their shady past to testify. Can you imagine what a thrashing a skilled defense attorney would put them through?"

"I think it would be best to lie low, hide the women, and develop a case that blows the lid off this city's sexual exploitation of women," I said.

"We all know corruption runs in this city," Al said. "People on the street openly complain about it. But no one fights it in the courts or in the press where it might begin to make a difference." Al's neck reddened with his intense concern. "And why is nothing done about it?" He slammed his fists on the table.

"The fact is whistleblowers in this city get crucified," Ron said. "The corrupt politicians and their lawyers have this uncanny ability to find something shameful in the whistleblower's past that discredits his testimony. Who wants to risk becoming a target and having his dirty laundry hung out for all to see? Do you want to end up looking just as bad as or even worse than the ones you accuse?" Ron asked.

"So, we need to reduce the shame of having our deep dark secrets exposed and increase the number of people willing to bear shame for the sake of others," I said. "It feels safer to be one of twenty prostitutes telling the story of their exploitation than to be the only prostitute speaking up."

"And it is much harder for lawyers to demonize twenty than it is to make a fool of one solitary witness," added Ron. "So, we need to make this case bigger than the exploitation of the four women under our care. Yes, there is shame in being a prostitute, but our whole community bears the greater shame of tolerating abuse and doing nothing to rescue."

"Are we biting off more than we can chew?" Al asked.

"Better to aim high and miss, than to aim low and hit," I said. "Since our plans involve the girls, we need to make sure they are up for it, but they're so tired. For now, we better let them keep sleeping."

"Agreed," a female voice announced. Heather entered the room from the tunnel. "The others are sleeping soundly, but I couldn't sleep. So here I am, eager to help."

"Welcome, Heather," Al said, barely glancing at her, and then returning to our planning session. "First, who are our opponents? Who would be damaged if we stood as witnesses of their criminal behavior?" Al asked.

"If not criminal, then at least scandalously inappropriate," I added.

Mayor Russell T. Molson topped our list, then came Police Chief Charles Alexander, followed by the fire chief and the police officer who tied up and tormented Ron behind the fire station. "That's the list for now, except possibly the two police who were hunting for Ron and me when we were hiding at the police community center," I said.

We determined which of us needed to stay hidden while the others were out in the community getting the information we needed for our case. Al could go back to his community center because publicly he had neither supported nor spoken against anyone involved. People who came to the community center would surely be talking about the mansion fire. Al might overhear valuable information.

"I've done some articles for the Free Press. The news editor and I are friends from way back," I said. "I'll see if I can get him to assign me to do a feature on the sex mansion, once things settle down, and I know it's safe. If so, I'll have a press pass to get more information we can use. For now, since I haven't been identified, I think I can move around, as long I lay low."

"How about you, Ron?" asked Al. "Is it safe for you to go back to work? After all, one of your coworkers threatened to murder you, and your chief was trying to strong arm you."

"Don't think I haven't thought about that." Ron leaned back in his chair and stretched his legs. "The good news is my friend, Pete, who recently retired from the Fire Department, has promised to be with me from the moment I leave home until I return, unless someone else, like Al here, is with me. Pete packs some heat. He carries a gun. So do I, even in my house, but still, I think it's less risky for my family, if I find another place to be. What if I stay here for the day, and then head out tonight under the cover of darkness to see my family?"

"What about us?" Heather asked. "What's going to happen to us?"

Al turned to face her, leaning toward her. "Do you have something in mind, Heather?"

"I was locked up for only a few days. It seemed like forever. I'm still restricted and that makes me desperate to be out in the world. Free! Who knows how long these women have been imprisoned? How much longer do you expect them to remain shut off from the world?"

"Just until we know they have a safe place to live and friends to be with them and protect them," I said.

"So, you think we need babysitters for the rest of our lives?" Heather's deep concern for the three women fueled her growing anger.

"Keep the volume down," I cautioned. "We don't want to advertise our presence here."

"That's another problem," Heather said. "Can you reduce four women to nonstop quietness? Do you have any idea how hard that is?"

As Heather went on listing her concerns, Al jotted them down. *I wonder if this is the first time a man took her seriously enough to write down what she was saying.*

"Thank you, Heather, for letting us know your concerns," I said. "When the others wake up, we'll find out more about each of their needs and then brainstorm the kind of resources and support they will need to meet those needs."

"I can tell you that my support is practically zilch," Heather reported.

"Think about it and see if you can find support that you have been overlooking," I said. "We usually have hidden support that can be immensely helpful. But we need to look for it. Just like this carriage house that we've discovered. It supplies a suitable place to rest."

"Speaking of support, let's start with what you need immediately. How are you doing for clothes?" Ron asked.

"Not so hot," Heather said. "Now that I've rested, I've realized how uncomfortable these soot-covered bodies and ripped clothes are."

"I agree," I said, "I am looking forward to getting into some clean clothes myself.

"I was thinking, Ron, since you need a place to lay low, that you could stay here with the girls while I made a quick visit later today to my house. I could grab some clothes for the girls and get some supplies for the next few days," I said.

" I think that's a good idea, and then I could head out tonight under the cover of darkness to see my family," Ron replied.

"I remember seeing a well outside. Let's look around for some buckets, so we can give ourselves sponge baths when the fresh clothes arrive. That will get us through the next day or two," I suggested.

"Speaking of cover of darkness, I want to get going before too many people start the day. I wouldn't want to alert people to the fact that you guys are here," Al said. "Ron and Dave, I will let your families know you are safe."

"Could you also let Pete know?" asked Ron.

"Sure. And Dave, you shouldn't be getting supplies. Even if you haven't been identified, they are still looking for someone of your description. I am thinking it makes more sense for me to grab them and bring them over to Kate and Jenna. That way when you think the coast is clear to get to your house, you could bring the supplies back with Kate and Jenna's help, so they could be here too," Al said.

17. Does Anyone Care?

Wednesday, April 4

After Al left, Ron, Heather, and I explored the carriage house and its surroundings.

"I found some buckets!" Heather exclaimed. "We could wash up using that well you found, Dave. When are you going to go get those clothes? How about now? I am getting tired of feeling so grungy."

"I wish I could accommodate you, but I don't want to leave the women without letting them get to know Ron first. Plus, it's getting busy out, I'll need to wait until the early afternoon lull to make my being seen less likely," I said.

It was late morning before the women sleepily staggered into the kitchen. I put another pot of coffee on and introduced the girls to Ron.

"I'm starving," Krystyl moaned.

"How about these granola bars that I keep in my backpack to give to the homeless? I guess we could be considered homeless," Ron quipped.

We all laughed.

While we ate our meager breakfast, I gave the three who had slept through our planning session a review of what we covered. Then I nudged the conversation toward freedom. What would that look like for them?

I could have guessed the lack of supportive people in their lives. Heather had a guidance counselor. Krystyl and Marta could think of no one. Ana felt uncertain about her mom, dad, and siblings. Would they welcome back the prodigal daughter/sister? One person she was sure would welcome her was her adoptive grandmother who lived in the mountains south of West Wend.

"She's kind and wise, a little too religious for my liking," Ana said between mouthfuls of her third crumbly granola bar.

"What does too religious look like?" I asked.

"She reads her Bible every day, I mean every day. She goes to church on Sunday, sometimes all day. She meets on Wednesday with a group of six or seven who pray for each other. She says they pray for me too. A lot of good that's done."

"Maybe it has done a lot of good," Krystyl said. "You're no longer a slave."

Ana groaned, running her fingers through her matted afro. "Right now, all I care about is getting cleaned up."

"I share your eagerness to freshen up. I am hoping to bring my wife and daughter back with fresh clothes and better food than what we've had so far. But it won't be safe for me to go until after the lunch rush," I said.

"Are you okay with Ron hanging out with you, he needs a safe place to hide too. Ron, why don't you let these women know why you need a hiding place?" I asked.

As Ron shared the story that revealed the danger he was in due to his trying to defend Heather, I could see the girls' faces warm to him.

Reassured by their trust in Ron, and eager to see my family, I left. Though it was still densely overgrown, the path that Ron and Al had cleared in their coming to the carriage house was navigable. *They've made it easier for our friends to get to us, but I hope our enemies don't find this route.* I put a few large branches to block the opening of the path, so that it wasn't visible to those who might be searching. Once out of the Mansion's 'backyard', the two-mile walk to my home took less than 20 minutes.

#

In my youth, I was a Billy Graham wannabe. One feature of Billy Graham's life was the frequent and lengthy absences from his wife, Ruth. She told inquirers she would rather have Billy with his absences than anyone else even if he was rarely home. My wife, Kate, and I respected Ruth for sacrificing time together with her husband to allow Billy to preach to millions around the globe.

My wife was just as generous and gracious when she learned how I was trying to help Krystyl, Marta, Ana, and Heather. I know men whose wives grumble, yell at them, administer the cold silent treatment, or in some other way give their husbands grief if they are absent or late, no matter what the reason. Not Kate.

She often opposes me, usually because I have overlooked important consequences. But when she knows that the mission is from God, she partners with me. And she knew that helping these four women was an assignment from God.

"I can't wait to meet them," Kate said. "They must be aching for a woman to listen to them and mother them."

"Is that your way of saying, 'It's time for the real work to begin?'" I said, sarcasm seeping from every word.

"Your sarcasm calls for recognition of all you have done for these girls." She stood on tiptoes, so she could put her arms around my neck and look into my eyes. "It's beyond heroic."

I wanted to soak in my wife's admiration. But my daughter, Jenna, kept things moving.

"Did you say that Heather is my age?" Jenna asked.

"Sure did. And she's smart like you and compassionate, but tough."

"Do you think she'll be good with guns like we are?" At age 12, Jenna asked for her own gun. She and Kate took gun safety courses and we three did target practice together once a week. During our target practices, Jenna and Kate hit the bullseye more often. By the time she was 15, Jenna rarely missed the central circle.

"She's your kind of person, Jenna. She's caring and wise far beyond her age, but also, a passionate pursuer of justice."

"Could we have Heather stay with us while she is trying to straighten things out with her family?" Kate asked while Jenna held her breath and nodded.

"I thought you would never ask, honey." I hugged her tightly. Jenna joined in to make it a sign of our family's unanimity in welcoming Heather.

"Did Al drop off supplies and let you know that we were hoping you two could stay with us at the carriage house?"

"Of course, we would be willing, and I added a few items to the supplies, that you men wouldn't think of," Kate teased.

#

Later that day, I returned to the carriage house with Kate and Jenna. The women enjoyed trying on clothes that they brought. They jumped up and down and giggled as Kate distributed the carrots, licorice, chocolates, and other items that Al had purchased.

The freedom I experienced in visiting my family, and Ron's anticipated return to his family after dark, created, within the women, a longing for the freedom to come and go as we were cautiously enjoying. We agreed after much dispute that Heather, Ana, Marta, and Krystyl should remain hidden until the older three broke free from their drug addiction and until we were sure they were protected from former clients, pimps, or relatives who might wish to see them working the streets... or dead. Meanwhile, the four had remained hidden from public view and so were presumed to be dead, we hoped.

"How can we be sure there is no one out there who suspects we escaped the fire and who is afraid we might expose him as an abuser?" asked Krystyl.

That question weighed heavily on all our minds.

18. Stunning by Stunning

Thursday morning, April 5

"Let's celebrate," Heather said, after breakfast was cleared and morning Bible reading. She lifted her hand as if giving a toast. Everyone followed her example. "To life and a fresh start... thanks to the Von Moeller family, Ron's family, and Al... even though we have to live like the Amish."

We all laughed.

"Shall we discuss plans for today?" Just as I said this, the front door reverberated with loud hammering.

My heart skipped a beat. Terror gripped tightly. Then with my finger to my lips, I pointed to the passageway behind the refrigerator. Like frightened chicks sprinting for shelter under their mother's wings, the women and Heather headed for the fridge.

"Kate and Jenna, stay with me," I said. "Kate, close the panel. And Jenna, push the refrigerator to the wall and lock the wheels."

"Why couldn't I go with Heather and the other women to the tunnel dormitory?" Jenna asked.

"Our visitors may have seen you coming here with Mom and me when we brought supplies." I answered. "They'd be asking where you two have disappeared to." I paused to make sure that Kate and Jenna had finished securing the fridge, then

I looked through the door's peep hole and counted five police officers. I threw the door open just when one of them charged forward to smash through the door with his shoulder. With nothing to stop his forward momentum, the thick-necked, heavily shouldered, bullish man stumbled across the room until he crash-landed face forward on a sofa.

"Make yourself comfortable, Skinny," I said with obvious sarcasm.

He turned and twisted his huge frame into a sitting position. "Argo!" he growled, then huffed and puffed his way to his feet.

Meanwhile, the other 'officers,' openly looking my daughter and her attractive mother up and down, shoved their way past us to fling open cupboard doors and pull out kitchen drawers. They dumped the contents on the counters and floor, scattering them around. I hadn't had time to close my laptop and noticed Mr. Skinny searching my history. *He's probably looking for signs of child pornography or something else to incriminate me.*

"Excuse me," I protested. "You're ruining a get-away with my family that we've been planning for months. You're way out of order—trashing this place! Are you going to take responsibility, and clean up this mess? But worst of all, you treat my wife and daughter with no respect. May I see your credentials?"

"Shut up and sit down," the bullish man ordered.

Ignoring his order, I stayed on my feet and shouted, "Who's in charge of you vandals?" Ignoring me, the men continued to rummage through our supplies.

No response.

Using my policeman's voice, I boomed, "Stop! in the name of the law."

It didn't faze them. They kept ravaging the household. So, I pulled out my taser pistol and ordered them to leave. Kate and Jenna drew their guns to back me up.

Surprise covered the faces of the younger officers, three of whom obeyed my order and fled. But a fourth one drew his pistol. *God, this is getting out of hand.* He lined me up in his sights. His index finger on the trigger. Then he hesitated.

My mind was racing. Should I try to beat his trigger finger and shoot him with my taser or try to reason with him? *He's pausing. Let's see if I can bring him to his senses.* "Do you want to be a cop killer and spend the rest of your life in prison?" I asked.

The would-be shooter's jaw clenched tightly as he weighed my question. But before he could think of how to respond, his boss answered for him.

"Don't shoot," Skinny, the fat man, ordered, his eyes drilling holes through the three of us as we stood confidently with guns ready.

He knows we have the drop on him, I thought.

"Let's go, Wade," the big man said to his recruit. And they exited, shuffling cautiously past us.

"We'll be back," Skinny warned, glaring menacingly at me as he paused in the threshold, then stepped outside.

"Nice of him to invite himself back," my wife, Kate, remarked as she went to bolt-lock the door.

"Stop! Kate!" I yelled, but too late as I saw Skinny spin on his heels and reach in and grab Kate.

From his pants pocket he produced a switch blade knife which he clicked open and held to Kate's throat, using her as his shield.

"I'm in charge now," said Skinny. "First, put all your weapons in the kitchen sink where one of my men will give them a bath before we leave."

He called his men back. "Get in here, you bastards." Skinny ordered. None responded.

"The way you treat those guys, it's no wonder, they don't obey you. As you know, it will go hard on you if you fail to show common decency," I warned.

"That's assuming you get out of this alive," Skinny chortled, and once again hollered to the four who remained outside. No response.

Are they reluctant because of the way Skinny treats them or do they realize they would be on the wrong side in this conflict? "I guess they're hard of hearing," I said.

"As bad as you. I told you to sit down and shut up."

"No, you didn't," I said with a snooty tone. "You said shut up and sit down. Which is it?" I hoped, by mouthing off, to enrage him against me, so that he would forget Kate and come after me.

"Damn you! I'll teach you to get smart with me," he yelled as he shoved Kate to the floor and lunged at me. I dodged. He grabbed at my arm to regain his balance. I twisted away, taking a few quick steps backward to regain my balance. Skinny charged at me with arms opened wide... *What a wingspan! I'm trapped.*

Then Jenna cut loose with a shrill scream that made Skinny flinch and pull back. In a split second I chose not to play offense, which meant getting close enough to receive punishing blows by kickboxing or slugging it out. *No way!* I want to avoid making him even more angry. So, I leapt over the table with the hope of keeping the table between us.

As Skinny came at me around one side of the table, I went to the opposite side. And so, it went for a few rounds. Meanwhile, I apologized for making fun of his command. "But you still haven't shown me your credentials."

"I don't need to show you anything except this." He reached behind his over-sized flanks to draw his gun. But his bulk made it a long reach, giving me time to pull my taser. As he raised his gun to put me down, I zapped him.

Skinny's face contorted into surprise, then shock, as he crashed to the floor in a rigid twitching heap. Knowing I had only seconds before he regained control of his body and two minutes or so before his confusion dissipated, I grabbed his gun.

Wade, hearing the scuffle, kicked the door open to investigate. Seeing his boss on the floor, he backed away, but not before I stunned him. I scooped up his gun and put both weapons in Jenna's hands. "Put them in the refrigerator," I smiled. "Maybe it will help cool things down."

"Stand by that wall." I commanded, pointing Skinny and Wade to the far wall of the living room. Still dazed and unsteady, they obeyed.

Having shaken off the aftershock of having a knife held at her throat while in the big man's vice-like grip, Kate retrieved her gun. "What can I do to help?" she asked me.

"Are you sure you're okay, Kate?"

"Yes."

"Then, do you have Al's number in your phone?" I asked.

"Yes."

"Ask him to bring enough officers to book five guys."

While Kate phoned Al, Jenna stood guard. I searched our captives and found another gun on Skinny's shin, in addition to the one he had tried to use on me.

"Kate and Jenna stand guard over these guys, while I go locate the rest of the guys," I said.

"We'll be trusting God to shield you as you round up the rest of them," Kate said.

A large but squat mushroom-shaped willow tree stood twenty feet from the carriage house entrance with leaf-lavished lower branches reaching the ground. It looked like if you got inside the wall formed by the lower branches, you could walk all the way around the tree, getting a 360-degree view if you peeked out by parting branches. The darkness provided by the tree's shade would hide you. *An ideal hideout! But what if one of them is hiding in that tree? Hmmm. Let's see if I can get them to reveal their location.*

I fastened my T-shirt to a long stick and stuck it out the door for a few seconds, then quickly pulled it back.

It took no more than a second for two shots to ring out, the first shot came from a brush pile straight ahead about fifty feet out. The second shot rang out to the right as you faced the carriage house near a giant spruce. *So, now I know where two of you are. And the bullet hole in my T-shirt tells me one of you is a sharpshooter. Probably the third guy is old and wise enough to hold fire and therefore not give away his location. He's probably in the willow tree.* I waited for a sign to tell me what to do. After a few eternal seconds I got my sign.

Cr-r-r-a-a-c-k. A branch of the willow broke under the weight of someone... progressively lower branches bent down, breaking the fall of someone... *someone must be the third guy.*

Taking advantage of this diversion, I sprinted from the carriage house to the tree. A volley of bullets followed me, one grazing my left arm. Once inside the shelter of the tree, I found the man who fell. He was grimacing while propping up his right hand and wrist with which he tried to shoot me. But he couldn't lift the gun. Shuddering with pain, he dropped the weapon. "Looks like a bad wrist sprain. Anything else injured?" I asked, as I scooped up his gun.

"Don't think so."

"Then, let's lie down in the hollows formed by erosion around these huge roots. That will protect us from getting hit by a stray bullet," I said. "And remain quiet unless I ask you to speak."

"I will."

"Help me Lord, please, to convince these last two to surrender," I whispered.

"Atten-shun:" I boomed. "I want the guy hiding behind the brush pile and the one by the giant spruce to listen up. Your commanding officer and the recruit called Wade have both been captured and are being held in custody along with a third deputy whose name I've yet to learn...."

"Don't shoot." The man from behind the brush pile eased out with his hands held high. The other man took off running and tripping through the brambles. My first shot missed him. *You are getting rusty*, I chided myself and sent off another round. The second shot felled him.

At that moment, Al arrived with his contingent of police and emergency medics. "Thank God, you're here!" I fist-bumped him, then launched into my to do list. "We've got one down with a bullet wound. He's over by that giant spruce. And he's armed. Two voluntarily surrendered. One's by the brush pile and another is under that beautiful old willow tree. He has a severely painful wrist injury." As soon as I had pointed out each location, two medics hurried to take care of the injured.

I asked Al to assign his best negotiators to the armed guy that I shot. Turns out, negotiators weren't needed. The excruciating pain from his lower leg canceled all other concerns. He traded his weapon for relief.

With the medics caring for the two injured captives, I told Al about the other two, whom Kate and Jenna had moved outside. They were seated on the ground in front of the carriage house.

"I've nicknamed the big boss man, Skinny," I told Al, as we approached the carriage house.

#

Outside the carriage house, things seemed oddly calm, putting me on edge. *Something's happening... What is it? Oh, I know. Skinny's mouth isn't threatening or demanding. He hasn't said a word.*

"How did you get him to stay quiet?" I asked.

"I warned him, either you shut up or I'll jolt you with another shot from my taser," Kate said.

"Nice of you to give him a choice!" I gave her an approving kiss to her forehead. Skinny's neck, purplish-red dispersing into blotches of red on his cheeks, told me how little he was enjoying the forced silence. By giving him a no-talk zone, Kate had given him a chance to think.

Curious to see if he had gained a healthier perspective, I said, "You can talk now, but only about what you have learned while using your eyes and ears instead of your mouth."

"You can't do this to me," Skinny bellowed.

"That's strange. It looks like I already did. And while I'm doing what you say I can't do, I'd like to know why you're searching this house, Skinny." I could see he didn't like the nickname. That's why I used it, to keep him on edge where his body language or words would be most likely to reveal his thoughts.

"Why should I tell you?" the big man blurted.

"How about this? You're showing signs of serious heart trouble—sweating, rapid shallow breathing, a pale face. If you don't get medical attention soon, it could be too late. But we're not taking you to an emergency room until you give us some information."

"Argh!" He half howled and half wheezed in frustration. Skinny nearly tripped over his tongue he was in such a rush. "We're looking for the prostitutes who went through the fire in the mansion and might've escaped to this carriage house."

"Is that what the mayor and police chief ordered?"

"Ye—" Skinny bit his lip and turned his head away. He couldn't have said 'yes' more clearly.

Supplied by Al's men, and with their help, we handcuffed Skinny, Wade, and the guy who came out from his pile of brush to surrender. Three of Al's men marched these three off to be questioned. And as for the two badly injured ones, they were carried by stretcher through the tangled woodlot, to ambulances that took them to the hospital.

Knowing full well that the police chief would likely release them, Al called out to them, "As much as you might be following orders from the top, we're following orders from Above. Be careful what side of the law you choose to be on. The right side will win eventually."

19. On the Run

Thursday, April 5

"The girls must be worried sick," Kate said. "I'm going down to tell them the coast is clear. Do you want to go with me, Jenna?"

"Of course." Jenna smiled at her mom.

Kate pulled the fridge out from the wall. Then mother and daughter followed the tunnel to the passageway that led to the room. The girls, hearing them coming, got up from their knees to see how God had answered their prayers.

"We heard a lot of scuffling, and it sounded like gunshots. Was anyone hurt?" Krystyl asked.

"Let's go upstairs and we'll tell you all about it," Kate responded.

Once they all emerged from the tunnel, we joined together in a huge group hug.

"We're dying to know what happened," Marta said.

"Everyone grab a drink," Kate said. "Then we can sit around the table and talk about it."

"Meanwhile, I'll call the guys who missed all the action," I said. "We need to figure out when we should move, since our enemies have found our hideout... I don't understand how they caught up with us so quickly."

As I arranged a conference call with our team, I heard snippets of Jenna's rendition of how we captured Skinny and his gang.

"Dad showed that tasers can be quite effective. First, he disabled and confused Skinny, who was attacking Dad. Then he jolted Skinny's sidekick into submission," Jenna reported.

While the women replayed my 'stunning' feats, making me out to be a 'shooting star,' I surreptitiously basked in the glory. But not for long. We had decisions to make.

Too restless to sit, I paced around the room while I talked to the guys on the phone. After a half hour of testing one another's ideas about what to do next, I gathered the women to tell them what we had discussed. "We all wanted to know what you think about our plans."

"If we'll be going any long distances, we need to keep in mind that three of us are going through drug withdrawal," Ana said. "We won't be able to go at a rapid pace."

"Let us know when you need to rest," I said. "We'll gladly take a break."

"But we need to be cautious. Through his contacts on the police force, Al verified that Skinny and Company were looking for evidence. They were wondering if you three women and Heather were staying with us at the carriage house. Since they came ready to use lethal force this morning, they mean business and are likely to come again with more force."

"How did they close in on us so quickly?" Kate asked. "It's like they can hear everything we plan."

"Speaking of plans, I haven't yet heard where we go from here," Krystyl said.

"Ron has been puzzling over that for a while," I said. "He told me yesterday he found three canoes beside the creek at the back of the carriage house property. Through his contacts in the property records department, he found the owner, who gladly permitted us to use the canoes and the carriage house. He told Ron that he was hoping his property could be put to beneficial use. Ron said to take the canoes downstream to the river where there's a stand of sumac in which we could hide the canoes and make our way on foot....."

"Hold it, Dave!" Kate anxiously interrupted, looking at her watch. "It's three hours before sunset. We need to eat and go while we still have daylight's help. So, let's keep talking while we fix and eat our last meal in the carriage house."

That's my wife. Because she sees the big picture, she knows what we need to do now.

Having eaten quickly and headed out, we fought our way through the woods' brambles, briars, and fallen branches, and arrived at the creek, only slightly bruised and breathless. After a few minutes of rest, we removed the branches that concealed three canoes, and the seven of us launched out into the creek. Wonderfully tall cattails lined the sides of the creek standing straight, like well-disciplined soldiers. What a contrast to our disheveled crew.

"Where will we stay tonight?" Krystyl asked after we had canoed less than a half hour.

"You'll find out soon." I pointed downstream to four hitchhikers standing on a dock with their thumbs out.

Silhouetted by the afternoon sun, their sudden appearance evoked frightened gasps. Ana stood, preparing to dive off the canoe. Marta grabbed her arm to restrain her.

"It's okay," I said. "They're our friends."

Waiting there to secure our canoes to the dock were Al, Ron, Pete, and Al's partner at the police community center, Joe.

"You gave us a scare," Marta scolded.

"That's for sure," Ana gulped, rubbing her sweaty palms.

"How did you get here?" Heather asked.

"Pete knew of this place where the creek borders a city park," Ron said. "So, it was easy to get down here. Look! There's our car." He pointed to Pete's Ford Escape parked on a nearby street.

"That's not fair," Heather complained. "We had to plow through brambles, briars, uprooted trees, and fallen branches to get here. We're exhausted! You guys drove down here in the comfort of a car?"

"You're right. It doesn't seem fair, does it," Al said with a fake smile. "But you try to cram four men my size into a tiny Ford Escape, and you might change your mind about whose journey was more unpleasant."

"Men!" Heather groaned as she whacked Al on his massive shoulder with her paddle. "You're like Little Caesar's Pizza—

always trying to be the 'ExtraMostBestest,'" she said with a silly side to side movement of her head while throwing air quotes.

"I guess I deserve that," Al said with a chuckle. Still smiling, Al introduced Joe, his partner from the police community center.

"I'm looking forward to getting to know y'all," he said in smooth southern diction. "I'll start by giving you a sample of southern hospitality. Two miles from where this creek empties into the river, my family owns a secluded waterfront cabin where you can stay until the end of May."

I gave out a low whistle. "What a stroke of luck! Thank you, Joe."

"Joe and I will join you, canoers, while Pete and Ron take the car to the house," Al said.

"We'll need more than luck if we're going to pull off this caper." Al navigated his canoe around a big rock. "I'm surprised Chief Alexander hasn't dogged us with helicopters...."

"How about drones?" Jenna pointed her lips to an object hovering about two hundred feet above us.

That wily schemer, he's probably been watching us ever since we left the carriage house. Does he have some high-tech tag that he's attached to one of us without that person's knowing it? Or is one of us a spy, reporting all our planned and actual movements? Either way, they've outsmarted us.

Sensing my uncertainty, Joe pointed ahead to a bridge under which we could find shelter while planning our next move. "Beach the canoes on that sandbar under the bridge. Those of us who have weapons, be prepared to shoot down that drone if it threatens us. The rest of you need to stay with your canoe under the bridge."

Al grabbed his gun. So, did I. With guns held high, we jumped into the water and watched the drone descend, laden with cameras and weapons, then hover over the far side of the bridge, waiting to attack when the group emerged from the far side.

A car passed over the bridge, the driver unaware of the drama unfolding. Al looked up and down the highway. No cars in sight. He took careful aim, squeezed the trigger, and sent a bullet on its way. The drone fell out of sight. I heard a splash. By the time I waded to the sandbar, Al, who had worked with drones for several years and knew them well, had deactivated its weapons and cameras and was starting to dismantle its GPS.

"We have a minor miracle here," Al said, "This is the department's best drone. We've shut down one of their most useful spies."

"But doesn't our shooting down the drone give him a real crime to accuse us of?" I asked. "Until now, the chief has found only fictitious crimes to charge us with. But now we're guilty of tampering with and stealing police weapons."

"It was shoot or be shot, I thought, so I shot the drone rather than letting it shoot us.... Let's talk about it later," Al said. "For now, we need to bend every effort to get to Joe's cabin before sundown."

We had been paddling gently with the current, but now we paddled strenuously to put as much distance as possible between ourselves and the last place where the now disabled drone had tracked us. We came to the tall stand of sumac bushes that marked the place where the creek flowed into the river. There, we hastily parked the canoes, and began walking upstream beside the river to Joe's place.

20. Skirting Around an Orgy

Sunset, Thursday, April 5

Sandstone bluffs lining the river had, through erosion, receded from the river edge, supplying a wide sandy beach for us to walk along. After walking a mile or so, we rounded a bend to find the beach occupied by noisy frolickers. If it's true that the more alcohol you consume, the louder your voices boom then the noise level told us the partiers were loaded.

Respecting their privacy, we stayed close to the bluffs as we skirted around the almost naked partiers. I wanted to flee, which is my usual way of dealing with overexposed women. But passing around this party was the only route to Joe's place. The men, like the women, seemed to be in a contest to see how much they could uncover and still be classified as covered.

Some experiences so profoundly tempt or delight or frighten us that they make an indelible imprint on our memory. They become our 'I'll never forget stories.' For example, I'll never forget the flattened head of my neighbor after a truck ran over him. When I recall his pancaked face, the same shock sweeps over me today as I felt back then, twenty-five years ago.

This journey through an orgy promised to be in the 'I'll never forget' category. I wondered if the other men in our group felt the tug that gripped me.

And God knows what our women were struggling with.

This unbidden rush of thoughts and feelings swept over me in an instant, making me feel like a criminal before I had committed the crime.

When we passed out of sight of the revelers, I dropped to my knees in the sand. "Lord, have mercy... What just happened?" I asked.

"I don't know about you, but I know about myself," Al said. "All those nearly naked women did me in. I feel like I've got to power wash my brain."

I saw a puzzled expression on Joe's face. "Let me explain," I said. "We guys have been talking about being faithful to our wives. We want to be one hundred percent devoted to them, which includes how we use our eyes."

"What do you mean?" Ana asked.

"I mean that although it's okay to look at a woman and appreciate her beauty, we want to refuse to entertain sexual desire for anyone but our wives," I said.

"Are you serious?" Joe asked.

" Yeah, I used to think that since the temptation to lust hits us in a flash, God would understand if we lingered, as long as we don't act upon our thoughts. But now I know, I need to immediately open my heart to Jesus." Al said.

"As Christians, we follow Jesus, who said, 'if you look at a woman with lust in your heart it's the same as committing adultery.' So, Jesus challenges men to have eyes only for their wives." I said.

"Wow! Are you kidding?" Joe asked.

"Think about this," I said. "Imagine a world where all married men were one hundred percent faithful to their wives. And all singles remained virgins until married. Would there be pornography and prostitution and aborting of unwanted babies ruining women's lives to satisfy the lusts of men?"

"Well... I get your point." Joe cupped his hands over his eyes, and in an almost mocking tone said, "Monkey see no evil.... But don't you guys, when you see a beautiful girl, wonder what it would be like to... You know?"

"You better believe I'm tempted," Al said. "But it helps me to hold back if I think of younger women as my sisters and older women as my mother or aunt."

"Knowing men's weaknesses, some women use sex for power," Ana said. "It's not just your money they want. They give sex to gain the favor or the influence of a powerful politician or to clinch a business deal. For them, sex is power."

"But security is what most women crave," Krystyl said. "Preferably the security of faithful love that Dave and Al are talking about. It blows my mind to think that a man could love me like that. But if a woman can't get that, then at least she wants financial security."

"And you get neither security nor power in the sex business," Marta said. "What you get is slavery and abuse."

Kate interjected, "I can't believe we're having this conversation, since some of us hardly know each other, and sex is so private. But if you want to know what I was thinking and feeling as we passed through that party back there," my wife said, "I was angry. I saw them as exploiters of one another...

certainly not lovers. True lovers don't give their bodies to just anybody. They save their bodies for the one they marry. Sex is intended to be the 'glue or adhesive' that powerfully binds the married couple together in a life-long exclusive joyous relationship."

"But if you're having sex with one person after another, it's like using tape over and over again. It loses its sticking power." I demonstrated with my hands. Clasping my hands tightly together and unable to part them, I said, "This is sex exclusively with your marital partner. It gives the couple the security of a permanent bonding. The bonding weakens if you have sex with more than one partner." I pulled my hands apart, with each successive time it became easier to do.

"That's small comfort to people who have been forced to have sex with a bazillion filthy-minded perverts." Ana rolled her eyes as she spat out her words.

"Here's the good news," Kate joined in. "If you fall in love with Jesus, he cleanses you of all unrighteousness, and he is able to heal you from the effects of your experiences."

"It would help us in our battle against sexual exploitation to know more about what you women have gone through emotionally, and what it has taught you," I said. "But for now, let's quicken our pace, so we can be at Joe's place before dark."

Sun-reddened clouds displaying heaven's glory were overtaken by lengthening shadows as Joe led us along the narrow path to his family's 'cabin'. "We've got another quarter mile to go," he said.

We walked on in silence, punctuated by 'oohs' and 'aahs' evoked by shooting stars. "Shouldn't the One who puts on this display get some credit for it?" Al asked.

"Yeah, I think he's way cool!" Jenna responded.

21. Drug Withdrawal

Thursday night, April 5

The 'oohs' and 'aahs' continued as we entered Joe's family's luxurious waterfront home. It certainly was not a cabin as Joe had called it. The living room must have measured thirty feet by twenty. Pull back an accordion-style divider and the dining room was completely open to the living room. Pull the divider to the closed position to have the dining room separate from the living room. The kitchen was open to the dining room with only an island suggesting a boundary.

Upstairs, the master bedroom contained a king-sized bed, covered by an elaborate quilt featuring fabric portraying sand dollars, starfish, driftwood, and other items tossed up on an ocean beach. The wall art continued the same theme.

"This walk-in closet is big enough to sleep four people," Kate observed. "And a Jacuzzi! This is too much!"

A long hallway led to four more bedrooms, three of which had a toilet, sink, shower, a queen-size and a twin-size bed. The quilts covering the beds in these three rooms reflected the theme of the room. The shelves in one room held a collection of miniature classic cars. Delicate porcelain dolls lined the shelves of another room. In yet another room, vases of all shapes and sizes adorned the walls, from cute and tiny vessels to two stately six-foot-tall Ming Dynasty vases guarding the door. A mountain scene gave the fourth bedroom a 'lost in the wilds' feel. Two twin beds and a bunk bed along with toilet, sink, and shower provided for four occupants.

"Dave and Kate can have the master bedroom. Jenna and Heather can sleep in the porcelain doll room next to them." Joe pointed to the rooms as he assigned them. "Al and I can enjoy the classic car room tonight. You three women can have the mountain room."

"We'll reserve the vase room for Ron and his wife, if she's free to come."

"I could get used to this," Jenna whispered to Heather.

"Not me," Heather replied. "It's too ostentatious, too many precious artifacts that I might accidentally break."

"What big words you use – os... ten... ta... tious... ar... ti... facts." Without a hint of sarcasm, Jenna stretched out the words to exaggerate their size. The two of them snickered, enjoying their linguistic elitism.

"But seriously," Heather said. "I love to use the word that most accurately describes what I'm talking about, especially if it's colorfully polysyllabic. You might say it's an obsession with me."

"I'll cogitate on that as we conversate," Jenna promised as Heather joined her in a playful high five.

# #

Ana leaned against the hallway wall, hugging herself and shivering. "I've got the shakes from withdrawal," she moaned. "And being without a fix frightens me."

"Speaking of drugs," Kate said, "none of you are writhing in the kind of pain withdrawal usually brings. Have you been hiding your suffering?"

"Till now, I've had nothing to hide, except for chills and a runny nose," Krystyl said. "But now I'm feeling like I have a bad case of flu. Every muscle in my body aches. I desperately need a fix."

"Me too," Marta said. "My heart is pounding, and I feel like I'm jumping out of my skin."

"And me three," Ana said. "We're all going through withdrawal."

"If you would like, you can lie or sit on your beds while we do what we can to help you," Kate said. "I'll go get some bottles of Gatorade. One of the most important things we can do is keep you hydrated so your electrolytes will be balanced."

"You talk like a nurse," Joe said.

"That I am," said Kate. "And as a nurse, I strongly recommend these women take the medical withdrawal option. They need special drugs to ease their withdrawal and they need medical specialists to oversee the process."

"But that would mean the women would have to come out of hiding," Ron said.

"So, we have two options," Krystyl said. "Quit cold turkey with no guarantee that we will remain safely hidden here. Or take the gentler withdrawal in some facility back in town where our pursuers are almost certain to find us."

"What do you wish to do?" I asked.

They hesitated. So much was at stake. Their very lives.

"Before you answer, let's talk with the One who knows and loves you more than you love yourself," Kate said.

Before anyone had a chance to pray, Marta scurried to the nearest toilet to upchuck.

"Lord, as you calmed the stormy sea, so settle Marta's stomach, and Krystyl's and Ana's," Jenna prayed. "And give them wisdom to choose the best method of withdrawal."

"I can't let them recapture me," Ana said. "I'm staying here, no matter what."

"We've come too far on the road to freedom to give it up," Krystyl said.

"I agree," Marta said, as she returned from the bathroom.

"I'll do my best to help you through this," Kate promised. "Why don't the rest of you go to bed? Dave and I will do what is needed to care for the girls."

Pete yawned and piped in, "I am headed out for the night, Ron, I will let your wife know you are safe and that a room is available if she wants to stay here. I will be back in the morning to take over, so Al and Joe can head out to work."

22. Celebration Breakfast

Tuesday, April 10

During the women's withdrawal, Kate mobilized us to supply what they needed to survive. Under Kate's supervision, we gave them extra strength Tylenol for pain, along with plenty of water, Gatorade, fresh vegetables, and broiled fish and high protein bars.

We prayed with them when the pain seemed to crush them; and reasoned with them when they became irrational. Mood swings scared us at first, especially when Ana became suicidal. We found that hearing the Bible provided a calming effect. The hymns and choruses of the church, such as *Savior, like a shepherd lead us* also effectively quieted anxious hearts.

By Tuesday morning, the women were feeling much improved. We invited all the guys who had assisted us over the last week to join all of us for a celebratory breakfast.

Using supplies from the generously stocked cupboards and refrigerator, Kate baked a coffee cake and frittata. Jenna prepared sausage and bacon. Heather fixed hash browns and coffee. When all was ready, we gathered around the large dining room table. After I prayed, we eagerly chowed down.

"Even though I caught only bits and pieces of what you were talking about while we ate," Ron said, "what I heard helped me know you better. And I thought it would be great for us to tell our stories so we would know each other better. Why not spend some time now telling our stories? If you want, I'll break the ice by going first."

"I'd like that," Kate said, "but what if someone doesn't want to do it?"

"They can pass," I said. "Go ahead, Ron."

"I was the oldest of six brothers and six sisters." Ron began. "My dad worked two jobs to keep food on the table. Because Dad was always at work, Mom was in desperate need of help. So, I helped my mom take care of my brothers and sisters. You can imagine how I envied the boys in the neighborhood. While they were playing basketball, volleyball, and, on rainy days, ping-pong, or bowling, I was helping mom run the house. It left little time for play.

"When I was ten, our house caught fire. All but my oldest sister got out. My dad went back in to save her. Both died in the fire.

"Mom had to go to work. My family needed me more than ever. I was a mere boy trying to meet the needs of my ten father-less siblings whose mom was often absent. God got me through it. And I'm probably a better man because of carrying a father's and mother's load."

"Mom and I organized the family, so that each one had chores to do. People admired how well we worked together, but I was the one to fix it if we weren't working together. I often asked men from our church for help in disciplining those who rejected my leadership or correcting me when I was too demanding. I don't think we would have survived if it hadn't been for the help our church gave us. They helped us reconcile our differences, fixed the toilet when it broke, paid off our credit card, visited to find needs they could meet, prepared meals for us, brought their kids over for game nights. What a good thing to be part of a loving church family!"

23. The Man Every Woman Needs

Tuesday, April 10

"I have at least one thing in common with you, Ron," Heather said. "We both lost our dads when we were children. My dad died when I was three. I don't remember him. My mom remarried when I was six." A long pause followed while she stared blankly at the table.

Heather dabbed her watery blue eyes and bent forward, looking to the floor. Her long blonde hair formed a round shield in which she hid her face. Then she uttered a sigh. With a flip of her head, she threw back her hair and sat straight.

"I've never told anyone, but my counselor tells me I should open up with people I trust... So here goes. From ages three to six, I was sexually abused by several of the men my mom dated. They all threatened to kill me and my mother if I told.

"My mom knew about at least some of the men. But when I tried to tell her, she would either shut me up or change the subject. The abuse was a dark secret that I had to deal with alone. By the time I was seven, I thought of myself as a prostitute. I felt dirty, ugly, used, and helpless. Oh, and yes, at that early age I knew what a prostitute was.

"My stepdad didn't touch me. His abuse was verbal." Heather bit her lower lip. Her chin trembled. "It makes me sick when I recall the labels that he plastered on me. So, I'm not going to repeat them. Not once did he say a kind word about me or to me. Even when I tried to commit suicide on my fifteenth birthday, he only sneered, 'We'd all be better off if you had succeeded. But you couldn't even do that right.'"

Heather began to shake, then came a sob and another and another until years of dammed up tears cascaded down her face.

Marta cupped her hands around Heather's shoulders and looked into her eyes. "Having that kind of cruelty heaped on you would destroy most people. How did you get to be such a bright, beautiful, caring person?"

"A friend invited me to her church where I met an incredible person. He was kind, loving, understanding.... But what mainly drew me to him was knowing the kind of friends he attracted— prostitutes, cheating tax collectors, farmers, fishermen, criminals, women, children. You should've seen how he played with children. They loved him. So, did I.

"I couldn't get enough of Jesus. The pastor's wife gave me a Bible and pointed out the books that told the story of Jesus. He was the man every woman needs. Along with Jesus, I could pour out my heart to the pastor's wife. I can't tell you the relief it was to know she was listening, caring, and helping me know how to deal with the craziness in my home.

"But wonderful as she was, having Jesus as my friend helped me the most. Let me tell you one of my favorite stories about Jesus. A bunch of Jesus' enemies tricked a woman into having sex with a man who wasn't her husband. They caught her in the act of committing adultery. Then they hauled her off to Jesus to see if he would do what the Jewish law required and have her stoned....

"I love the way he put people in their place. He said, 'Whichever one of you hasn't sinned go ahead and stone her.' They all slinked away because they knew that if they were exposed as they had exposed this woman, they would be ashamed.

"But here's the part I like best. It's when the hypocrites left Jesus alone with the woman. He asks her, 'Where are your accusers? Are none left to condemn you?'

"She says, 'No one, Lord.'

"Then Jesus says, 'I don't condemn you either. All I ask is that you stop sinning.'

"Can you imagine that? I picture Jesus standing face-to-face with me and saying, 'There's nothing you have done that I haven't already forgiven. All I ask is that you accept my forgiveness and stay close to me so I can teach you how to overcome sin in your life.'"

"Overcome sin?" Ana asked. "You're no sinner. You're kind, thoughtful...."

"Oh yes, but I am a sinner," Heather said. "For example, I know Jesus wants me to forgive my stepdad and I can't do it."

"But that's understandable," Ana insisted.

"Understandable disobedience is still disobedience," Heather said.

"Whoa! You're too much, girl." Ana sat back in her chair. "I just can't buy it."

24. Marta — The Last Time I Cried

Tuesday, April 10

"I can't buy it either." Marta ran her fingers through her straight, red hair, the black roots exposing their original color. "It seems wrong to forgive cruel people like Heather's stepdad... or like the people who sold me into slavery when I was a little kid.

"My earliest memory is of a woman hugging me, crying, saying goodbye. She puts my hand in the hand of a woman in a tight business suit who then puts me in a cab and gets in beside me. I begin to cry. I stand on the seat so I can see the woman who gave me away. But she buries her face in the chest of some guy. She's weeping now. I want her to look at me. She turns away. I cry and cry and cry. Oh, to see her face once more but all she gives me is her back. I keep watching, hoping she'll turn as the distance grows. Finally, I see her no more.

"Was the woman who gave me away my mother? Possibly. Was the man I last saw her with my father? I don't know. Maybe. How old was I? About three. I knew only Spanish words, so I assume I'm from somewhere in Latin America. But I don't know. I relive that memory of parting every day but come no closer to the answers to the questions that haunt my soul.

"The lady who took me let me wail a little while, then without warning, she screamed, 'Stop crying, you tiny bitch!' I cried even more. So, she slapped me across the face so hard it

136

made the bones in my neck pop. It took my breath away. That was the last time I cried. I went into survival mode.

"The lady delivered me to a shed behind a large farmhouse where about thirty other girls and I spent our days and nights herded into this hell hole that had been a shed for cows. It reeked! We used five-gallon buckets as 'toilets.' Pity the person who spilled a toilet. She not only had to clean up the mess but was beaten up by her fellow prisoners – or were we slaves? One thing for sure, we were trapped in a world that only Satan could have invented.

"The sadistic guards, called 'aunties,' randomly chose one or two of us per day to torment. When my day came, the auntie was furious over something... she dumped the crap and pee of a toilet on my head. To add mortification to humiliation, she forced a fellow prisoner to rip off my dress and made me use it to clean up the mess. The aunties were bent on breaking us. I'll never forget that feeling of being defiled.

"I don't know how many days I stayed in that shed. Occasionally, someone came to take one of the girls. None of them ever came back. After a while, the lady in a business suit appeared again. She took me to a motel where she scrubbed my hair, soaped me until my body was white with suds and red from rubbing. She then showered me and repeated the process. She put me in new clothes. All this, with barely a word. She must've known the horrors of the system she was sending me into. I hate her!

"No little girl should be forced to fulfill a man's sexual fantasies. I'll not describe what I went through. Just let your mind go wild with sexual experimentation and you'll barely begin to know what juvenile sex slaves endure.

"Some men were gentle and avoided painful activities. Others acted as if I were just a body to experiment on. Sometimes, those experiments hurt. Always, they added a heaviness to my hatred of myself and my abusers."

Marta spoke without visible emotion as if describing washing dishes. I wondered if her three-year-old self was still holding to the vow to never cry again. I felt tearful rivulets making pathways down my cheeks. I imagined Marta as a frightened little girl being so cruelly abused. I looked around and saw others sniffing and wiping away tearful streams with the back of their hands.

"How did you survive?" Kate asked.

"One of the older girls told me to use my imagination to escape to another world. That worked sometimes. Other times I memorized the man's face, promising myself if I escaped, I'd track him down. Then I'd tie him spread-eagled to a fence and mutilate him."

25. Krystyl — Satan's Slave

Tuesday, April 10

Krystyl shook her clenched fists in the air. "Like Marta, I want payback. I dream of tormenting everyone who molested me. I want to make the brutish devils who have violated me go through the tortures they heaped on me. Also, like Marta, I'm from another country— Cambodia. My parents were poor. They moved from Cambodia to Thailand, seeking a better life. But my father found only low-paying jobs.

"One day, Dad brought home a customer he met in the shop where he worked. The man had asked Dad to describe his children— how many he had, how old they were, and what they looked like. Dad said, 'Of my three beautiful daughters, my eight-year-old is exceptional.' The man said he'd like to see me.

"Extending typical Cambodian hospitality, my father invited him to our house. The man told my parents that I could be a model and earn a lot of money. He said I would earn enough to bring our family to America. You can imagine how excited we were. And as icing on the cake, the man even gave my father one hundred dollars.

"The next day, I went with the nice man from our home in Pathum Thani to Bangkok. Although my city was near to Bangkok, I had never been to Bangkok. The crush of traffic frightened me as cars and motorcycles competed for space. With horns blaring, vehicles darted from one opening in the traffic to another, totally disregarding lane markings. It was each man for himself. Bangkok traffic became a picture of my life. I was pushed and shoved from one place to another, unable to escape the endless noise and crushing push of men.

"The man who bought me said I would need training to be a model. 'Some of the things the trainer asks you to do will seem strange,' he said. 'But the more quickly you learn to do exactly what the trainer asks of you, the sooner you can take your family to America.'

"Walls surrounded the trainer's house, as was the case with most of the houses of that neighborhood. The trainer led me to a beautiful flower garden behind her house and asked me to walk through it while she photographed me. For the second walk-through, she taught me to swivel my hips. With each walk-through, she introduced more seductive moves until she had me stripping off all my clothes as I walked. I felt uneasy, but I was determined to do exactly as told so that I could get my family to America.

"The photos my trainer took of me must have stirred up interest, because soon I was featured in live shows that played in the red-light district. Doing a striptease in front of sex-craved men frightened me, but I wanted to help my family go to America. Wasn't our family promised that? So, with dreams of America dancing in my head, I performed exactly as taught.

"But my dreams never came true. I never saw my family again. Sure, I got to America, but at what cost. By then, I had serious doubts about the nice man's promises. Still, I did pretty much all that my owners told me to do. Why? Because I had seen others severely beaten or tortured for not cooperating. I froze every time I heard their pitiful cries.

"One day, I heard my name mentioned in a shouting match between the women who oversaw us, so I listened.

"'It's time for Chouma to be having sex with our clients,' the owner said.

"Chouma is the name my Cambodian and Thai 'mothers' gave me," Krystyl said. "It means refreshingly beautiful. 'Mother' is the name we gave to the women who oversaw us.

"'She's only ten,' my 'mother' protested.'

"'We start most girls at age eight,' the owner said.

"'But most girls aren't porn stars,' my mother responded. 'Do you realize how much money her videos make? People from all over the world are buying them. Each new video brings in more new fans. We'd be fools not to use her in porn until she's fully developed. We can make a whole series of videos that show her all the way from eight to sixteen or even eighteen. Those videos alone will make more than turning her into a prostitute ever would.'

"When I heard their plans, I tried to escape but quickly learned how far and wide the net spreads to capture those who run away. I didn't know anyone. Didn't know where to go. Had no money for a bus or cab. They kept me isolated and ignorant. I was almost relieved when they found me wandering the streets. My punishment for trying to escape was harsher than I could have imagined. If they needed to keep me beautiful as a porn star, they couldn't hurt me too badly, I thought.

"Wrong! With ropes around my ankles and wrists, they tied me to the four corners of a table. They encouraged the other girls at mealtime to mock me. But that wasn't all. One of the mothers, a chain-smoker, snuffed out her cigarettes on the soles of my feet. Talk about pain!

"'You can't escape from us,' my so-called mother sneered menacingly.

"I still can't walk far without the pain returning. You'd think pain with every step would turn me into a rebel. But it had the opposite effect. It scared me into being even more compliant."

Ana frowned. "More compliant? Does that mean you performed kinkier sex?"

"I guess... you could say that, " Krystyl said hesitantly. "Until I was 16, I never completed the sex act. We faked it in the videos we made. But I did oral sex, performed all kinds of sensuous dance moves. I did whatever the movie director wanted. And I acted as if I loved doing it. I desperately wanted to please my owners.

"Just before I came to America, my owner told me why they kept me from going all the way. 'We want to keep you fresh so the buyers will pay more.'

"I thought I'd seen everything, but the transition to adulthood plunged me into the pits of hell. My pimp tricked me into taking drugs. Soon the drugs created in me a demanding emptiness that only drugs could satisfy. So, it was either obey my pimp and get my fix or disobey and get beaten and suffer withdrawal. Since I almost always obeyed, they gave me a steady supply of drugs and what my owner thought was a cushy job. He rented me to a Satanic society.

"I cleaned places of Satanic worship before participants gathered. And I cleaned up after their gatherings. They did not allow me to attend their masses, which they celebrated at night, candles providing the only light. Hidden behind a door or drapes, I sometimes stood in the hall where they assembled, listening. The speakers denied heaven, hell, and the need for a Savior. They mocked the idea of loving one's enemies. They said if someone hits you, hit him back harder. 'Only the spineless lets himself be hurt without retaliating.' They often rocked the building with stamping and shouts of praise to Satan.

"Their worship involved blood sacrifices. Sometimes menstrual blood. Very messy. A former Satanist told me that sometimes they sacrificed human infants. But I never saw that. I did scoop up, once, what I'm pretty sure was a baby's finger. It was in the blood left after a very intense worship service. The sight of that tiny finger pointing at me sickened me with shame. Shame for my part in a world that made casual sex stylish and virginity ridiculous. Shame that I didn't ask for but felt every time a man used me. Shame... Here comes my deepest shame. Shame that I hadn't done all I could to save the babies my owners forced me to abort. Why didn't I try harder? Often, when I let myself think about what they forced me to do, I feel physically sick to my stomach.

"Meanwhile, the Satanists I had to serve thought nothing of it. They worshiped gods who gave them power and pleasure. And they seemed to be powerful people who enjoyed all kinds of pleasure, including pleasure that they took from me."

Ana jumped up from the table and started pacing the floor. "I hate to interrupt your story, Krystyl, but I can't stand it," she said, shaking her head until her tight black curls sprang up and down, creating a lively frame for her bronzed face. Pain-hardened worry lines in her forehead and around her eyes revealed her fear. "I'm troubled about the pain you have endured, Krystyl. But I am also feeling extremely anxious. The city's chief officers and their lackeys are hunting us down. They have probably already found us and they're just playing with us like a cat torments a mouse. And we sit here telling stories. We need to do something."

"I doubt if they would try to arrest you, that is, if they suspected you were here," Joe said. "They know this is my family's house. I'm sure that out of courtesy to me, a fellow cop, they would contact me before raiding my home."

How can Joe be so sure, I thought. *Is he on the police chief's side?* Not wanting to cast doubt on such a congenial host, I kept quiet, but took note of my growing suspicion.

26. Ana — Child Seeking Way Home

Tuesday, April 10

"I still think it won't be long before they find and close in on us," Ana argued. She hugged herself, shivering, feeling the aftershocks of drug withdrawal.

"You might be right, Ana, but so far we haven't found a place safer than this," Al said. "In addition to celebrating the remarkable progress of your withdrawal, we plan to explore today various options for your employment and housing that are more likely to be safe."

"Before you talk about a more permanent place of safety, Al; I would still like to hear your story, Ana." Kate stood behind Ana, massaging her neck and shoulders. "Would you like me to stop?"

"No, the massage feels good. Do it as long as you like."

"I'll do it if it helps you share your story," Kate said.

"Oh, so you're manipulating me?" Ana huffed.

"Maybe," Kate chuckled.

Ana took a deep breath and sat up straight, readjusting herself under Kate's kind touch, "You could title my story *Stupid*," Ana said. "I came from a loving home... Had two brothers and three sisters... Mother and Father loved us... I went to church... Sang in the choir... Did well in school... Spent summers as a counselor in a camp for inner-city kids. I was the oldest child. My siblings were model teenagers except for my younger brother whose wildness and curiosity led to his joining a street gang. He was shot and killed in a gang war, while I was away at college.

"Friends in college introduced me to marijuana. It was stupid, I know, to try it. 'Just once,' I told myself. It went against all that my parents taught me, but I liked weed and it seemed harmless. Everyone in our group smoked it.

"Then one day, our supplier gave us something new-- heroin. Talk about a step up! I was hooked at once, along with five of my other friends.

"Unlike most drug users, I had no sad childhood. I was never abused or neglected by my parents. I was seldom treated unfairly in my family. You could point at nothing that would drive me to drugs unless, maybe, I was trying to numb myself from the pain of my brother's death or wanting something I didn't have in my relationships with men.

"I longed to hear a man say I was beautiful." Ana hesitated and bit her lower lip. "It never happened. Not on dates nor from the guys in my group of friends. Just once did I have a man who said I was beautiful, but I soon found out he only wanted sex, not me. So, drugs were my substitutes for the lovers I never had.

"I flunked out of school. Couldn't keep a decent job. Sold drugs to support my habit. I was ashamed to seek help from my family. A friend told me about this place that provided addicts with all the drugs they needed if they took part in a research study. It was a lie. They locked me in the cubicle where you found me.

"Then you show up, Dave and Kate. In the brief time I've been with you, I've seen your love for one another and somehow your contentment with Jesus' love. Before my exposure to you folks, I had sworn that I was done with Christianity. I could feel my face stiffen when someone mentioned Jesus, God, or prayer. It was too easy and fun to be sarcastic when it comes to anything religious. But underneath, I think, I am a child crying to find her way home."

Kate leaned over and hugged Ana tightly for a long time.

Home! In normal families, home ranks among the highest treasures of one's heart, I thought. Happy thoughts filled my mind as I reflected on warm memories of home. It's a refuge where I'm listened to, appreciated, loved, defended, and challenged to go out and do my best. When home is ripped away or distorted as it has for these friends, it's as if all that matters is destroyed. Yet these women have not given up.

27. Women: Re-creating

Tuesday, April 10

I broke the silence. "How can we respond to your sorrow, your pain? It's so penetrating. Your stories... Heather, Ana, Krystal, and Marta have helped us know you. We will never be able to comprehend what you have gone through, but you've shown us enough to make us marvel at your strength. That you are still alive blows my mind. It proves that God cares for you."

"When we have gone through great suffering, we can let it destroy us or we can be like the oyster who responds to the irritating grit by transforming it into a pearl," said Kate. "God uses many ways to carry out this transformation. Reading God's Word and doing what it teaches is one way. Participating in activities that are re-creating is another way. I suggest that we women spend the rest of the day making 'pearls.'"

We all got up from the table, stretched, and carried our dishes to the kitchen. Because everyone helped, it only took fifteen minutes to restore things to order.

"Hey, girls, let's meet in ten minutes in the large sunroom at the back of the house," said Kate.

#

Heather bounced into the sunroom, shaking out her long blonde hair. "We need to move. We've been sitting around all morning."

"I agree," Marta added. "I'll be the leader. Everybody line up."

Lots of giggles went with the 'ups and downs' of the calisthenics. Soon the girls were breathlessly plopping down on the cushioned sunroom chairs.

"That was fun," panted Krystal.

"That was recreating," added Kate. "Now each of you think of something you enjoy doing or creating."

Krystal ran her fingers through her short black hair. "That's hard. I've never been able to choose what I would enjoy doing."

"I used to enjoy working with my mom in the kitchen," Ana said. "It would be fun to bake a batch of cookies."

"I've always wanted to learn how to bake. Can I help you?" Marta asked.

"Of course."

"In high school, I really liked art class, especially drawing and painting," Heather said.

"The other day, Ron brought over art supplies. I saw some acrylic paints and pads of paper," Jenna broke in. "I like to do that too. Let's go find them and see what we can create."

Krystyl moved around uneasily in her chair. "I don't know what to do."

"When we haven't had the chance to discover what we are naturally good at and enjoy doing, we can discover it by trying different things," said Kate. "I have yarn and crochet needles in my large handbag. I've been crocheting small projects while I've been helping you all through withdrawal. Why don't I teach you how to crochet a small coaster? You can see whether you like doing that or not."

28. Men: Fighting Sex Trafficking

Meeting of Al, Joe, Ron, Pete, and Dave,

Tuesday, April 10

While the women were engaged in much-needed recreational activities, the men settled in the living room to explore options for the women's future and to plan a campaign against sex trafficking. Al had learned that someone had informed the police chief that the women were too sick to go anywhere. "The chief hasn't bothered us because he didn't want to deal with the messiness of withdrawal," Al told us.

"So, we can expect to be hassled now that the women are better?" Pete threw his hands in the air in exasperation.

"Yes, but we have no way of knowing when the next round of hassling will begin," Ron said. "So, while we're all together, I'd like to see how committed we are to abolishing sex trafficking."

*I am relieved that the topic has turned general, with Joe here.... I don't really trust him to be involved in any specific plans for the women's future...*I mused.

"I've read dozens of articles on sex trafficking, but knowing Marta, Ana, and Krystyl has stirred me to action," Al told the group. "I believe God has called these women into our lives to mobilize us to stand with them against this horrendous curse.

"We've been engaged in small skirmishes in the war against sex trafficking," Al continued. "It's time to think bigger. I'd like us to aim for releasing every woman trapped as a sex slave in Asbury County. Let's make it so difficult and costly for pimps and johns to operate in our county, that they'll quit or go elsewhere. We're talking about a full-scale war on buying and selling sex."

"What do you mean by the word 'johns?'" Ron asked.

"'John' is the name commonly used for men who buy the services of prostitutes," Al explained.

"What does a full-scale war look like?" Joe asked.

Al proposed a media blitz that named the local johns and pimps and other people in the sex trade. "Buyers of sex, especially prominent ones, such as Mayor Molson, would be exposed," Al said. "Since the conventional media are under the thumb of the establishment, our information will need to be broadcast by flyers to be delivered to each household. We could build a website, too, and inform people through blogs, email, newsletters, social media, and other kinds of notifications. The total annual amount of money paid for illicit sexual services and products would be estimated, so citizens could know how big this business is."

"How are you going to get all this information, Al?" I asked.

"A band of journalists, like those trained by World Journalism Institute, who do careful research and are passionately committed to truth and therefore won't print hearsay or one-sided propaganda," Al said.

"But investigative journalists like that don't come for free." Pete rubbed his thumb across his fingertips. "We will need funding for sleuths who dig up the facts about sex trafficking in our county, showing the size and complexity of the problem. We will need funding for writers and speakers who mobilize word-of-mouth campaigns in every precinct."

"Then there's lobbying and pressuring lawmakers to pass laws that punish buyers and sellers of sex but acknowledge as victims and slaves the prostitutes and porn artists who want to escape but can't."

"Right, Ron." Pete nodded his head vigorously. "And we need to elect leaders who believe in our cause. Al, you said you wanted to know how committed we are to the fight against sex trafficking. Count me in for the long haul," Peter said.

"Me, too," Ron said without hesitation.

I looked at Joe who gripped the arms of his chair and stared at his white knuckles. *He fears he'll be the only holdout. I better cut him some slack.* "I need to talk this over with my wife," I said.

Joe wiped sweat from his brow. "And I need to talk it over with my girlfriend," he said.

29. Krystyl's Battle With Demons

Tuesday, April 10

We continued planning our attack on sex trafficking but were caught off guard by a frightening interruption. Krystyl began bobbing and weaving and thrusting out her fists as if boxing. She clobbered Kate, who had been exploring the idea of forgiving her abusers and leaving vengeance to God. Then she began talking to creatures who to us were invisible. Was she hallucinating?

"Leave me alone," she shrieked. "Yes, I want to torture the lecherous predators who defiled me," she continued talking angrily with beings we couldn't see or hear. "No, I don't want your help... I'll get my revenge on my own... they can't stop me...."

I surmised that demons were telling her she was too weak to resist Kate's appeal for her to forgive her abusers, and that she needed their demonic powers if she planned on getting revenge.

In her work with the Satanic cult, she must have dabbled with the demonic.

Krystyl had mentioned trying to curse her 'customers', hoping that they would miss appointments due to sickness or other problems. But it was hard to know whether a customer's failure to show was due to Krystyl's curse or something else such as bad weather.

Krystyl lashed out in every direction, hitting several, including me. I was surprised by the strength of her blows. "No, I don't want to go with you," Krystyl sounded like she was pleading more than declaring. She began shaking, suddenly turning pale. Marta and Ana tried to calm her, but the moment they touched her she violently pushed them away. She screamed, then falteringly tried to describe her feelings. "It feels like... a huge snake... is encircling my body... and crushing." Her every breath sounded like a death rattle. Suddenly, her hands flew to her throat, gripping it hard. It looked like she was trying to strangle herself, all the while fighting for air, and making a gurgling sound. *We're going to lose her,* I thought.

"Quick, gather around her. As you see, she's under attack. We need to form a wall of protection around her and trust Jesus to cast out the demons attacking her." I motioned for us to form a circle.

Kate began singing *"Jesus, Jesus, Jesus... there's just something about that name."* Others joined in singing, *"Master, Savior, Jesus... like the fragrance after the rain...."* As that chorus ended, Jenna began—*"Would you be free from your burden of sin? There's power in the blood, power in the blood. Would you o'er evil the victory win. There's wonderful power in the blood... of the Lamb."*

Calm settled on Krystyl as we sang song after song, filled with Biblical truth.

I told the story of the man afflicted by many demons who lived among the dead in the cemetery. "Jesus cast out all the demons that had controlled the man for years," I said, "and peace filled the man who had been so wild that he snapped the chains that people used to constrain him and ran around naked among the tombs.

"This same Jesus is here in this room, Krystyl. He wants you to trust him to cleanse you completely by his soul-cleansing blood. Trust him to fill you with his Holy Spirit who will give you power to break the chains that have held you."

It wasn't a pretty sight because the demons of self-hate, vengeance, self-pity, vanity, and despair tore at her as they fled from the presence of Jesus. She felt wrenching pain as they departed, but "It was as if Jesus' hands were finding every wound, and healing all that had been damaged," Krystyl told us.

"What about vengeance?" Joe asked. "Did he take away your understandable desire to get revenge."

Silence. It was as if she was searching through her heart. Then she smiled broadly. "Yes! The demon of revenge no longer controls me. I'm free. Free to love even my enemies, like Jesus loved that despicable man who lived among the dead."

We celebrated Krystyl's deliverance and Christ's presence and power that was working in all of us. Well, not quite all... Joe approached me while the others filled the place with laughter and excited talk.

"I'm not comfortable giving credit to someone who lived two thousand years ago. So, I think I'll leave the place in your hands for a while. Besides, I have a young lady I'd like to visit. I'll see you in the morning."

"You ask good questions, Joe. It *is* hard to believe that someone who lived two thousand years ago could cast out demons or somehow heal a person as broken as Krystyl was.

You can't help but ask, 'who or what healed her?' Modern counseling technique or God or both?"

"Those aren't my questions." Joe muttered as he walked hurriedly out the door.

"May I cut in for a moment," Heather's commanding voice rose above all the competing conversations, and the partiers paused.

"I don't like breaking into our celebration, but although we've won hard battles, we're consistently losing our battle against the demons behind the police chief and mayor. We can't shake them. So, let's use the momentum we're celebrating to increase our faith in God's power to overcome Satan in City Hall."

"I think we've been fighting well, but not realizing it." Ron put his Pepsi down and stretched his arms wide as if to gather us all into his embrace. "City Hall leaders have tried their best to get evidence against us, but the more they try to hurt us so that we do something stupid, the more evidence they mount against themselves."

30. Talk of Rehab

Friday evening, April 13, 2018

Alaskan weeping cedars formed a dense boundary around Joe's parents' twelve-acre property, providing peaceful privacy. Beyond this natural enclosure, wooded hills gave an opportunity for exploration. We enjoyed playing volleyball, badminton, and horseshoes. In the evening, we gathered for our usual Bible reading, which included "We wrestle not against mere humans, but against spiritual powers in high places."

Heather read that statement aloud and asked, "Isn't that what we were doing in our battle against the demons that attacked Krystyl? Weren't we fighting warriors of Satan's evil kingdom?"

"What do you think?" Kate asked. "Did you feel them even though we couldn't see or hear them?

"I did...so did I"...Almost everyone said they encountered unusual fear, dread, even panic. What a relief to enjoy peace after looking to Jesus, our all-powerful deliverer.

"I hope we've seen how necessary it is to depend on God in all we do, because only God can defeat these mighty powers, which oppose us," I said. "And he has assured us of his superior power in the battle he won for Krystyl."

"I am not so sure that we are anywhere close to winning the battle against the demons behind Police Chief Alexander and

Mayor Molson. I keep thinking about our future, and that it isn't safe to stay here," Ana said.

Before we separated to go to our bedrooms for the night, Marta spoke up, "I know you want us to go to a live-in rehab. But we want you to know that living with you, Kate, and your husband and daughter has been far better for us than any rehab we could imagine. You've shown us what a normal family can be."

"We've watched you argue without tearing each other apart. You always say, 'attack the problem, not the person.' We've seen how you do it, consistently," Marta said.

"You let Jenna fully express her opinion. And, sometimes, you choose her way over yours," Heather said.

"That's because she's right many times. Often, she's seen something that we have overlooked," I responded.

"And I love the way you read the Bible together every day and let God speak to you. It's like you're conversing with someone alive right here in this room." Krystyl swept her arms around as if touching the God who fully encircled her.

"I'm glad we've been helpful." Kate couldn't hide her tears. "It means a lot to us. But for your complete recovery, others can do much better. You need a clean break from this city where dangerous people know you and would like to either kill you or trap you in the drug and sex scene again."

"All that to say, we've found several rehabs," I said. "Here's a list with their websites. Check them out. Tell us which ones you like. We will talk about it tomorrow."

31. Girls' Untimely Departure

Saturday, April 14, 2018

I awoke the following morning around 4:30, stumbling my way into the kitchen for a glass of water, and feeling uneasy. The note on the dining room table confirmed my anxiety. "Get up, everyone," I yelled. In five minutes, all were gathered in the dining area. I asked Kate to read the note.

Dear friends, how can we thank you enough for giving us Life as it should be? You have shown us how to live through very tough circumstances. But now it's time for us to face life on our own— with God's help, of course. Thanks for helping us get started. We'll take it from here. And we hope you, freed from the burden of having to help us, get your life back soon.

Krystyl, Ana, and Marta

"They just made our job much harder," Al said. "Until now, the women were with us, so that pursuers had to go through us to get to them."

"We were a shield for them," Kate said. "If their pursuers find out the women have skipped out on us, they can mount a huge search party, backed by helicopters, hounds, and superior manpower without us being in their way."

"With a big search party, they're sure to get to the women before we can," Jenna said. "So, the longer we can make it look like the women are still with us the better."

"How do we look for the women without looking like we are looking?" I asked. "That's the question."

"Maybe we should use a decoy," Kate said, "like going back to normal. Return to our jobs, our homes, our normal life. That would suggest that we found a safe place for them, so the women are no longer in need of us. We could go our usual ways, implying that we had accomplished our mission and were confident that the girls were safe."

"I am beginning to suspect that Joe might be an informant, but I can't say for sure. As a precaution, we need to keep this note to ourselves, and tell everyone else, including Joe and Pete, that a rehab had called and had openings for all three, so we took them there overnight," I said.

Breathing out a deep sigh, at my implication that his partner couldn't be trusted, Al said, "You can trust me to keep all this to myself, I wouldn't want to risk the women's safety."

"It just occurred to me that I've been thinking that the women won't make it if we're not with them to protect and guide them," Ron said. "Didn't God teach us yesterday to trust in the superior power of his love and protection?"

"Merciful Father, thank you for Ron's reminder that *you* are protecting and guiding our somewhat reckless friends," I prayed. "Lead them to where they can heal, grow in wisdom, and learn to love you wholeheartedly."

"I'm feeling uneasy," Kate said. "We need to get back home if we want it to seem like we're done protecting the women."

After my family and Heather had returned home and had a chance to sleep in a bit, I called Joe with the 'news', thanking him for his hospitality, and informing him that Al was still at the beach house to help him lock up.

32. Rescuer Rescued

Sunday, April 15, 2018

A phone call woke Kate and me in the middle of the night. It was Krystyl.

"Can you come and get Marta and me?"

"Of course! Where?" I suppressed asking about Ana, knowing Krystyl might not have time to explain.

"What's going on?" Jenna wound her headband, tied it tight, and knotted it as she walked into the living room.

"132 Harbor Circle, Dexter," Krystyl spoke softly. "Locked in the basement. Guard in the living room watching TV."

I reached for my belt containing lock-picking tools. "Kate, I think you should stay here with Heather. Jenna, you're my driver tonight. Let's go." I directed Jenna to the expressway south toward Dexter as I fastened my seatbelt. We drove in silence until Jenna asked, "Are you scared?"

"Krystyl's voice was hushed. Sounded like she was scared. So, I assume we are walking into danger. Of course, I'm scared, but I'm also relieved that Krystyl and Marta are back in touch with us. But then, I'm worried about Ana. Where is she? How's that for a confusing answer?"

"For a man, you are unusually in touch with your feelings," Jenna responded.

"Truth is most men are in touch with their feelings. It's expressing or describing them that men find hard to do. They're more likely to do it with a woman who doesn't try to fix them. You're that kind of woman, Jenna. You listen because you really want to know the other person," I said.

"Thanks, Dad. I want to live up to that high compliment."

#

Harbor Circle formed the boundary of a residential area down by the riverfront. Almost swallowed up by surrounding high-rises and office buildings, these grand old homes represented resistance to dull modernity. The building numbered 132 was the spacious old home nearest the river. I got out just after we passed it, having instructed Jenna to wait for my call at the all-night Burger King two blocks away.

I walked up the driveway of the house next to 132. The gate at the side of the house was unlocked, so I slipped through and shut it. Padded feet approached, accompanied by a low growl. I kept dog treats in my pants pockets for just such occasions. Doing a quick reconnaissance through my pockets, I selected a roll of beef jerky which I held out to the dog. Taking it, he gave me unlimited access to his kingdom.

To my surprise, the back door was not locked. *This is too easy. Do they trust their dog that much? Or is this a trap?* I wondered. I checked my phone for the time. It was four o'clock. *Only a little over two hours of darkness to hide us. Trap or not, I gotta keep going.*

The back door opened, but not without a loud squeak. I froze and waited. Seconds stretched into minutes or were they hours? ... I could hear a television blasting. Common sense prevailed over my hyperactive imagination and told me the television drowned out the noise of the door's squealing, so I entered cautiously and descended the stairs to the basement.

Once in the basement, I saw several rooms with doors ajar. I went to the only closed and padlocked room. "Krystyl, Marta," I called in a loud whisper.

"In here," they responded. Just then I heard movement on the floor above.

"Someone might be coming," I said. "I'll be back." I slipped behind an open door at the farthest end of the basement just as I heard footsteps coming down the stairs.

Through a crack, I saw a huge man, all muscle, walking directly to Marta's and Krystyl's cell.

He opened the door and threw Krystyl to the floor. "Don't move," he commanded. He handcuffed Marta to a large metal ring attached to the wall. Then scooped up the struggling Krystyl under one arm, leaving the door open.

"You and I are going upstairs to try out some new moves," he said.

As soon as I heard them going up the stairs, I picked Marta's handcuff, setting her free. "Are there any more of their people here?" I asked.

"Boris, the big guy, is the only one here as far as I know."

"How about Ana?"

"I'll tell you when we have more time," Marta said. "She's not here."

We tiptoed up the stairs to the first floor. "Can you point me to where Boris took Krystyl?" I whispered.

She pointed to a room with a shut door through which I heard sounds of struggle.

"Marta, take the road out front to Burger King. You can see it from the front of this house. Jenna is waiting there. Wait with her. Now go." Marta left and I headed for the closed door that hid whatever Boris was doing to Krystyl.

As I approached, I could hear hard breathing and grunts. I opened the door about a half-inch. Boris's back was to me. He was grabbing for her, but Krystal was artfully dodging over and around a queen-sized bed, keeping the bed between Boris and herself. *She's amazing!* I paused to marvel at how this small woman was outmaneuvering this giant. Her flushed cheeks and heavy breathing told me she couldn't keep up the performance much longer.

I swung the door open and spun into a flying kick to the back of Boris's head. It knocked him down, but not out. His face registered shock as he turned over to confront me, I landed an even harder kick to his mid chest. He tumbled back.

"Get out, Krystyl!" I yelled as I landed a fierce kick to the groin. He doubled over, holding himself and groaning.

Krystyl headed toward the basement door.

"No, Krystyl," I said. "Marta has already escaped. We're going out the front, headed to Burger King...." I didn't have to urge her. She sprinted ahead of me.

A shot rang out. Thud. The bullet smacked into a tree limb just above my head. "Get down behind that hedge," I said. "Duck as you run so he won't see you." I looked back to see Boris coming after us, aiming his gun in my direction. A second shot rang out. Then I fell with a hot stinging pain in my shoulder. That's the last I remember. I awakened in piecemeal fashion. First, my sense of touch told me I was lying on my back, in a bed. It smelled like a hospital. I could hear, long before I felt able to open my eyes. I heard Jenna telling what happened while I was knocked out:

"I heard shots, so I took Dad's revolver from its hidden compartment in the van and prepared it for use. Marta and I then drove slowly down Harbor Circle. Along the way, I picked up Krystyl. I didn't see Dad with her, so I asked her where he was.

She told me that she thought he was right behind her. But neither of us saw him.

I grabbed Dad's gun, then we three plunged through the hedge and found him lying there out cold and bleeding. Before we had a chance to respond to Dad's needs, Boris approached with gun in hand. "How convenient," he said. "Not two, but three recruits, and the pleasure of knocking off this dirty fighter." In the time it took Boris to swing his weapon around to point at Dad, I drew Dad's gun and shot the gun out of Boris' hand. He grimaced as he looked in disbelief at his empty hand.

Holding Boris at gun point, I saw that his wound was not bleeding profusely. Dad, on the other hand, was losing quite a bit of blood.

Keeping my eye on Boris, I asked Marta and Krystyl if either of them knew how to stop wounds from bleeding.

"A nurse taught me how to slow my friend's bleeding from a bullet wound," Krystyl told me.

"Good, see if you can stop or at least slow down my dad's bleeding," I said.

Not seeing a clean cloth, Krystyl asked if she could use my bandana. I ripped it off and gave it to Krystyl who shoved it into the shoulder wound, pressing down on it as hard as she could.

Meanwhile, I watched Boris as he bent over to pick up his gun with his left hand. While he was bent over, I shot him again, aiming for the mid-thigh on the side opposite his hand wound. Despite my being an excellent sharpshooter, somehow my shot went astray, hitting him in the middle of the back. The big man crumpled to the ground as if his spine had snapped. When I drew near to snatch his gun, I saw him struggling, but unable to move his legs to get up. I wondered what I had done. Was he paralyzed? It couldn't be! I froze in disbelieving anguish.

"I need you to help me get your dad in the van," Marta yelled. The desperate fear in her voice brought me back to the danger Dad was in. Since Krystyl had to keep applying pressure to the wound, it was mainly Marta and me and adrenaline hoisting Dad into the van. Krystyl climbed in beside Dad and continued applying pressure to the wound.

I drove. Marta rode shotgun. We raced down the street that led to the freeway. Flashing lights! Sirens! "Yippee! I snagged a cop." I pulled to the curb.

I lowered my window and shouted: "We need a police escort to the hospital. We have a man bleeding badly from a gunshot wound."

"Let me see," the police officer said. He opened the back of the van that was wet with Dad's blood. "You're right. He needs help fast. Follow me." The cop ran to his cruiser.

I shoved the gas pedal to the floor, squealing away from the curb and, within seconds, I was crowding the cop as he climbed the ramp to the freeway. Another police cruiser joined us on the freeway, so we had sirens blaring and lights flashing before and behind us. It was scary but thrilling!

Thoughts of Boris slipped in to dampen the excitement. I remembered I had promised him an ambulance, so while we raced to the hospital, I asked Marta to call an ambulance for Boris.

"Why not let him bleed out and die?" Marta asked.

"I'm doing what my dad would do— giving him another chance. Dad always holds on to the hope that someone will change for the better."

"Forget changing Boris. We need to spend all our prayer on your dad, who doesn't need changing," Marta said.

"Still, I want you to give Boris the help he needs," I said gently. And Marta honored my request, calling an ambulance for Boris. I realized I had forgotten something. I told Marta that we needed to call mom. I knew that she would want to be by Dad's side the minute he arrived at the hospital. I told her to take my phone and put her on the speakerphone.

I told her that Dad was hit by a bullet, was unconscious, and bleeding badly, but that Krystyl had stanched the blood flow. Police were escorting us to St. Luke's Hospital.

Mom must have really been cranking, because she arrived here only a five minutes after we did....

#

Three hours later, I woke up with what seemed like a crow pecking away on my skull, producing a penetrating, pulsating pain. My wife had been combing my hair with her fingers when she found a lump the size of a tablespoon.

"Ow," I reacted. "Probably hit the brick sidewalk when I fell, which most likely is what knocked me out."

"Feel this?" Kate said, guiding my hand to my shoulder.

It was bandaged. "What damage was done here?" I asked.

"Surprisingly little, but the bullet nicked an artery, which explains all the bleeding. They have repaired the artery."

33. Jesus, Friend of Sluts

Sunday, April 15, 2018

"Where's Ana?" I asked as everyone gathered around my bed.

"As you know, Ana was troubled because she thought that she, Marta, and I were a burden to you guys," Krystyl said. "Marta and I tried to persuade her to wait until we found a rehab or at least a safe place to live. But she was anxious to leave."

"I don't know why we let her persuade us," Marta said, "but she can be a powerful negotiator. Our main motivation was to stay together. And at least she had a plan— to go to her grandparents in a small town thirty miles downriver. She planned to borrow a canoe from you folks and use it for transportation."

"We didn't count on how hard it would be to paddle all that way," Krystyl said. "We weren't using the current efficiently. We argued about how to paddle, whether we should stop and rest... We had spent a restless night, and then we had taken that long walk to where the canoes were hidden. By the time we got to the next big town, we were exhausted and starving. Ana was still holding out for continuing the journey. Marta and I refused to go on. What we didn't see was the audience we were attracting."

"How often in early Spring, when the river feels icy cold do you see three women who don't know how to paddle in a canoe splashing each other? We must have looked comedic as we drifted down the river, pulling against one another, yelling at one another, and accidentally slapping or spraying one another," Marta said.

"A police car pulled up to the edge of a dock. With bullhorns, the two officers told us to land, so we started trying to paddle towards them. We didn't think about the possibility that West Wend's Police Chief Alexander would put out an all-points bulletin, describing us as fugitives from the law. Every police officer in the region was looking for us."

"When we heard one of the men on the phone asking for Police Chief Alexander, it was too late." Krystyl pulled her hand across her throat as if cutting it. "The trap was sprung, we were captured, except for Ana. She stood and said, 'Love you guys, but I can't take any more of this life.' Those were her last words. Then she jumped."

"Jumped? Into the river?" Kate gasped.

"And drowned," Marta said.

"Ana? Dead?" Kate gasped, pressing her fists hard against her chest.

"Oh, God. No," Heather moaned.

"Should we continue telling you what happened?" Krystyl asked.

Sobbing, Kate nodded.

"Do you have more details?" asked Jenna.

"It was so unexpected and sudden, we didn't have time to stop her," Krystyl said. "Ana had tied her suitcase to her waist, so that when she jumped, the weight of the suitcase held her at the bottom. Both Marta and I jumped in after her, hoping to untie her and bring her to the surface. The water was too deep and murky. We couldn't see her."

"When we resurfaced, one of the cops was firing shots into the watery grave Ana had chosen. 'Stop!' Marta screamed. 'You should be diving in to rescue Ana, not trying to make sure she's dead.'"

"What made matters worse was the arrogance of the cops," Krystyl continued. 'Not even an idiot saves shit,' the cop in charge said. 'And a slut is worse than shit.' He sneered. His friends snickered."

"I lost it," Marta said, "so I told those cops: 'You got one thing right. Being a slut is worse than shit. That's why they mocked Jesus, because so many of his friends, if not sluts, were shitty. Jesus welcomed those shitty people. But he didn't stop there. He made them new. He's doing that for me. He'll do that for you....'

"'Shut up, bitch,' the cop in charge said. 'I don't need you, or your Jesus, messing with me.' He turned on his heel and walked to his car. 'Book them,' he hollered over his shoulder as he got into his car and squealed off.

"The cops didn't book us in Scottsville's jail, which is where they caught us and what we wanted," Marta continued her account. "Anything was better than being under Chief Alexander's jurisdiction in West Wend. All they had against us was stealing the canoe. And since our friend, Al, a police officer whom they knew, assured them over the phone that we had borrowed the canoe, they had no reason to hold us.

"But to appease Chief Alexander, who wanted us locked up until he regained jurisdiction over us, they sent us to the home of one of the local police officers who said he had a 'secure' room for us. You can imagine our shock when our host locked us in a prison-like room in the basement of a brothel."

"That's when we called you, Dave and Kate," Krystyl said. "And you know the rest of the story."

"How did you make the phone call?" Kate asked. "Didn't they search you for a phone? Besides, wouldn't jumping into the river kill your phone?"

"Not if it's in two ziplocked bags," Marta said. "And you have to get intimate to find where it's strapped. Fortunately, our captors were too polite to find it."

34. Vengeance? Hard to Let it Go.

Sunday, April 15

"You'll never guess who I saw being wheeled down the hospital hallway while I was out getting coffee," Krystyl said.

"Boris," Jenna said.

"How did you know, Jenna?"

"I guess it's because I can't get him off my mind." Tears gathered in her eyes. "I feel conflicted about him. When I shot him, I was beyond furious at the pimps and johns and others in the sex trade who brutalize women. I wanted to emasculate and ruin sex for all of them just as they had ruined sex for the people they abused. Here was my chance to keep at least one of them from ever hurting a woman again."

"You were not only punishing Boris," I said. "You were protecting me, your friends, and yourself. Boris was about to pull the trigger that would've killed me instantly."

"I get that, Dad. And I'm okay with the protection part. It's the punishment part that troubles me, especially the vengeance I feel. I hope I've inflicted Boris with permanent damage. It's nothing compared to the life-long trauma men, who like Boris, dump on the women and children they use."

"That's heavy," Kate said. "If you follow your feelings, you'll hate Boris and everyone in the sex business. But from somewhere inside, do you sense something that makes you doubt your vengeful feelings?"

"Maybe. But, Mom, his finger was on the trigger. He was calling Dad a dirty fighter... saying he was thrilled to send him to hell."

"If I were there, hearing Boris say those things, Jenna, I'd want to kill him, too." Kate pulled her daughter close for a long hug.

At last, Jenna spoke. "Would you have killed him?"

"I don't know what I'd do in circumstances like that," Kate said. "But if I found revenge in my heart, I'd ask God to forgive me. Believe me, it would be hard. But it would be the right thing."

"Why is the right thing always the hard thing?" Jenna asked.

"You know the answer to that, Jenna." Kate hugged her daughter tightly.

"Yes, the right way is hard because the right way is God's way. And we are all sinners bent on doing things our way. It goes against our selfish nature to do it God's way."

"Speaking of God's way," Kate said, "do you know why the Bible tells us that we're not to try to get revenge?"

"Why?"

"Because to take revenge you must judge that a person deserves punishment and that you're the one who should punish him. But do you know all there is to know about that person so that you can make a fair judgment?

"Let's use Boris as an example. Do you know his future? What if he gets sick of hurting women and devotes the rest of his life rescuing women from sexual slavery?"

"That's not a fair example, Mom, because statistics show that men like Boris don't change. So, you're supposing a magical never-never land. Besides, you've jumped to the future which no one knows."

"Wow, Jenna, you know how to mount a solid argument!" Kate broke the hug she had been sharing with her daughter and held her at arm's length, searching her face as if for the first time. "You argued well, but you missed something, the God factor. The God who transformed Saul, the hate-filled persecutor of Christians, into Paul, the greatest promoter of Jesus and his people, could transform Boris, too."

"I know I should ask God to forgive me for nursing a vengeful spirit," Jenna said. "But it would feel so phony."

I took Jenna's hand. "Sometimes what feels right is wrong. And what feels wrong is right. It's right to forgive, but it feels wrong (phony). So, you have to go against your feelings to do what's right. You have expressed well, Jenna, what we all feel. If we went by our feelings, then fueled by hate and revenge we'd hunt sex traffickers down and imprison them for life or kill them or castrate them. But instead, the Bible tells us to leave the punishment of evil to him and to work through our governments to outlaw and punish it. Meanwhile, we seize opportunities to rescue those trapped in this evil system, which includes praying for the transformation of sexual abusers."

I motioned for everyone to gather around my bed where we prayed for the women and children enslaved and terrorized by sex traffickers.

"And loving Father, teach me to love like you," Jenna prayed, "which means loving our enemies. Yes, replace my hate for Boris with your saving love."

#

While Kate helped me check out of the hospital, Marta, Krystyl, Heather, and Jenna visited Boris, as crazy as that seems. They took the elevator down two flights to the second floor with its highly buffed tile flooring. They couldn't tell for sure, but it looked like Boris was sitting in a wheelchair at the far end of the main hall. The color combination of burgundy from the floor to the handrails and sky-blue from there to the ceiling gave the impression of walking on God's good Earth and looking to the sky above. Jenna wondered if it had any effect on Boris. She bought a soda for him from the vending machine as they approached.

When Boris saw Jenna, he growled and tried to rise, but fell back, winded by the effort. His strong upper body worked just fine, but his lower body didn't. Even so, he struggled, like a mad dog leaning hard at the end of his chain.

"You bitch," he said, his face and neck reddening. "I will walk again. And once I've recovered, I'll come after you to rape you over and over again, then I'll cut you into a million pieces and feed you to my dogs."

"You cut me into a million pieces, and every piece will shout, 'I love you, Boris, because Jesus loves you.'" Jenna said.

"What kind of nonsense is that?" Boris scoffed, rolling his eyes, yet his face showing a flash of befuddlement.

"The kind of nonsense you'll find in Jesus and his followers," Jenna answered. "We love our enemies."

"'You pick a strange way to love— paralyzing me," Boris sneered. "I'd rather not have that kind of love. Now get away from me," he said with a menacing growl.

"You were going for your gun," Jenna said, "intending to murder my dad and make three women sex slaves. The bullet from my gun saved you from being guilty of murder and sex trafficking, horrible crimes to have on your conscience. Maybe it was loving of me to save you from committing such crimes."

Jenna approached Boris, being careful to keep his tray between them, which kept her outside his reach. Quickly, she placed the soda on the tray and turned to leave. Boris hurriedly opened the can and hurled the soda at her. It slammed into the side of her head leaving its contents dripping down her white shirt and khaki pants. Jenna simply smiled at Boris.

With that, the girls left to tell Kate and me about their conversation with Boris.

"Well, Jenna, you left him with something to trouble his mind," I said. "Good job."

"I doubt if he'll think twice about what I said."

"Who knows?" Kate said. "But here's a chance to trust God for what seems impossible— Boris' joining God's family."

"I'm curious," Krystyl said. "Why bother with people like Boris? Why not leave them be? It seems like you people are on a crusade to get everyone into your camp."

"You are right. We are trying to convince everyone to follow Jesus," Kate said. "The Bible tells us God doesn't want anyone to perish. He wants everyone to become part of his forever family."

"So, you believe God loves us all, and wants all of us in his family," Krystyl said. "Can you imagine Hitler and Mother Teresa holding hands and walking down the road as brother and sister?"

"Dictators, like Hitler, are too arrogant to bow their knee to Jesus. So, I doubt that they'll be in God's forever family. But I do think we'll be surprised by who is included and who is not."

35. Jailed

Sunday, April 15, 2018

Two squad cars awaited our homecoming from the hospital. *This can't be a celebration of my return,* I thought. *I know too much about Police Chief Alexander's questionable activities. So, this isn't his welcome back. Almost all these cops are young. I don't know most of them. My buddies on the force would never be a part of this. It's another trap.* I jumped out of the car and made for the house. Two officers stopped me. "Can you help me?" I asked.

"Depends," the young officer said. *How right you are to mention 'Depends', because...* "I've gotta pee... really bad or my Depends will overflow."

"Sorry, but you are going with us downtown to police headquarters." The obviously annoyed officer grabbed my arm and started to pull.

"I'll go with you. But let me relieve myself first. I have no control over my bladder," I said. "And I don't want to pee in your car."

"Fine." He spat a wad of tobacco at my feet.

It took a second to recover from the young cop's insulting arrogance. But my almost bursting bladder took precedence over my pride. It was no time for getting into a protracted argument. The conceited cop stuck out his chest and stretched his body to its maximum height, which was still shorter than mine, and scolded: "I'm adding resisting arrest to all your other crimes."

All? How many crimes do they have me committing? I wondered if I should ask but decided not to. I knew the older of the two officers. I knew that he, too, had an enlarged prostate and knew the weak bladder control that comes with it. I directed my appeal to him.

"Even if you label me an arrest resistor, I beg you to let me go to the bathroom."

"Okay," he huffed impatiently.

"But we're going in with you," the younger officer demanded.

"Be my guests," I said.

Upon entering our house, I realized why they didn't want us to see inside. They had searched our house, leaving it in shambles. I'm sure they wanted to be gone when we discovered what they had done. Kate, who had stood silently with me throughout the bathroom ordeal, moaned as she calculated the time it would take to put things back in order. I groaned as I headed to the restroom. The younger cop started to go in with me, but the older one held him back.

"Don't try to escape out the back window," he said. "You'll be picked up by cops stationed there."

In the ammo compartment of my very ordinary police belt, I carried some extraordinary items that could be useful if I were imprisoned and needed to communicate with someone on the outside. I was especially fond of high-tech tools. My friends jokingly referred to me as the most overprepared cop on the planet. But this time I brought only two items, because I thought my captors could find and confiscate other items. In the folds (excess skin or flab) that hangs loose under the arms, especially of old people, I taped my tiny lock-picking tools under one arm and mini cell phone under the other. Although the loose skin hid the items I was sneaking into the jail, someone carefully feeling would find what was hidden from the eyes. *Let's hope whoever checks me in is careless or God blinds his eyes and numbs his skin, preventing him from feeling or seeing.*

When I came out of the bathroom, I understood more fully what dismayed Kate. My bladder pain had minimized all other discomforts, but now I let myself feel the chagrin I experienced as I surveyed the mess they had created. "Did you find what you were looking for?" I asked sarcastically.

"Do you think we would tell if we did find evidence against you?" the young officer asked in a snarky manner.

There! You told me your agenda. You believe I'm guilty and you're looking for evidence to prove it. I glanced at my wife who gave me a shut-up-and-be-careful signal with her finger to her lips.

The police shoved me into the back seat of an SUV. I made as if I used up all the remaining space. So, they left me alone in the back. While they took me directly to their boss, Police Chief Charles Alexander, I dialed my wife with my mini cell phone. This opened the phone line between my wife and me, so she could hear and record all that the chief said to me once we arrived to his office. And it wasn't long before he got to the point.

"Mr. Von Moeller, I have reason to believe you don't like me and want to get rid of me." The chief rubbed the smooth, manicured tips of his fingers together. "I don't mind people not liking me. That goes with the job. But I don't take kindly to anyone who tries to undermine my authority."

"What makes you think that I'm undermining your authority?" I asked, returning his glare with equal intensity.

"I've looked at your record as a police officer. You were known for being a maverick, pushing the envelope." He grabbed from his desk a file folder labeled 'Von Moeller.' "I came on the force as chief five years ago and you quit shortly thereafter, calling me a racist."

"I have been cautious in my use of that word, 'racist'," I said. "All I did was to state the facts. You appointed no Black people and only one Hispanic to the force's key committees. Minority officers got the lowest jobs with the lowest pay. You relegated women to clerical work. Their complaints about sexual harassment went unheard. That's the way it was when you took over the force. And it is still unchanged. No. It's gotten worse because minorities and women have quit in protest." I took a deep breath, wondering if I should say what I was thinking, given the deepening redness of his face. *It can't get me into more trouble than I'm in already.* "I don't have to undermine your authority. You by your racist, sexist, and self-centered attitude have effectively eroded any respect this community might have had for you."

The redness in the chief's face deepened into purple. "How dare you question my administration like that?"

"I dare because I care," I said. "I want you to change for the good of your employees and the whole community. You could start by listening to your women employees' sexual harassment complaints and disciplining the perpetrators. But no, you won't do that, because you are, in fact, the worst of the harassers."

"You bastard. You're messing with the wrong man," he said, slamming his fist on the desk. "I could have you and your foul mouth silenced once and for all." He jammed his finger into my chest.

"Is that a threat?" I asked, facing him squarely.

"Let's say it's an option. You can imagine how difficult it is to control prisoners. Things have gotten out of hand. And people get hurt."

"Thanks for the warning with its not so veiled threats," I said cynically.

"For now, I'll set you aside in solitary confinement."

"For what crime do I receive such a privileged position?" I asked.

"Kidnapping, endangering the welfare of a minor, helping prisoners escape from police custody, threatening a police officer for starters," Chief Alexander said.

I was tempted to refute each charge but knew Chief Alexander wasn't about to listen. "I get one phone call," I said.

"No, you don't."

"When it gets out that you refused my right to a phone call...."

"Oh, all right. Just one call."

Making a show of using a prison phone, I called Kate. To my great relief, everyone was still at home. But the women still being under Kate's shelter hadn't come without a tussle. "I asked the police if they had a warrant for their arrest," Kate said. "They couldn't produce one, yet still persisted in taking the women. So, I told the women to scream at the top of their lungs— 'We've committed no crime. We won't do time.' And they kept shouting until the neighbors poured out of their homes. When they saw me trying to prevent police from dragging the women away, they converged on the police, questioning what was going on."

"I would have never thought of that, Kate. You scared the police chief's novice recruits into thinking they'd cause a riot if they forcibly took the women. I salute you."

"You should have seen the neighbors chanting while the police huddled together, looking confused. At least thirty people from further down the street watched in puzzlement. I told the police that until they provided a warrant for each one's arrest, we would not comply with their demands."

"Did they accept what you said?" I asked.

"I'm not sure. They seemed confused. They retreated to their cars. Then I had one of my inspirations." Kate chuckled.

"I don't know if I'm going to like this," I muttered.

"Why end on a sour note?" Kate asked. "It occurred to me that these recruits might someday be on our side in our battle against pornography and prostitution. I asked Heather and

Jenna to bring out drinks, which we gave to the recruits as they were leaving."

"Way cool," I said. "Kate, you're a genius."

On that note, Kate ended the conversation with me. She later told me that she made her way to the living room where she collapsed into a recliner, took a deep breath, and called our lawyer. She later recounted the following conversation:

"Did you say Dave is in solitary?" The attorney asked.

"Yes, why?"

"It's just that the last guy in solitary went in healthy and came out dead."

"Do you have any more good news?"

"Spoken like a battle-toughened warrior," he said.

"Not really. It's just the tough shell of bravado covering the jelly of cowardice," Kate said.

"I'll see what I can do about bail and visitation," the lawyer said. "Anything else?"

"Don't you want to know why Dave is on the police chief's hit list?"

"Not now. First things first. First, we get him out... Whoops. I've got calls coming in on three lines. Got to go." Click.

36. Spy Among Us

April 19, 2018

I made a big fuss over my right to make a phone call when I was booked into prison so that the police chief wouldn't imagine I had other communication options. What he lacked in imagination, he made up for, by psychologically and physically jerking me around. He piped into my cell angry rap — Eminem and worse —as well as the sultry whispers of women's voices inviting me to every imaginable hedonistic behavior. Overwhelming!

I knew that doing what the seducers suggested through their graphic descriptions of unrestrained debauchery, spelled surrender to the satanic. I feared that in a weak moment I would give myself over to the dark side. In my desperation, I rehearsed over and over what St. Paul wrote to his Greek friends living in Thessaloniki:

I want to learn more and more of the life that pleases you, my God, I know your plan is to make me holy, and that entails first of all a clean cut with sexual immorality. I choose to learn to control my body, keeping it pure and treating it with respect and never regarding it as an instrument for self-gratification, as do pagans with no knowledge of God. I know, God, that you will punish all who offend in this matter and that you are calling me not to impurity but to the most thorough purity, and if I make light of this matter, I'm not making light of man's ruling but of Your command. It is not for nothing that the Spirit, you, my God, give me through my faith in your son, Jesus, is called the Holy Spirit.

#

One benefit coming from the demonic noise pumped into my cell was that it covered the sound of phone conversations I had with my wife and others, especially Al.

I discovered that Al was a genius at seeing all that needed to be done for the success of what he called the Pure Pleasure (Political) Party. At first, I objected to the name. "Your 'pure pleasure' makes me think of unfettered erotic pleasure—pure pleasure," I told Al.

"Precisely," Al replied. "It gives our people a chance to show how evil elements, such as the illicit sex industry, have hijacked our vocabulary. Pure used to mean holy, perfectly clean. Pleasure was a wholesome delight. One front in this battle against impurity is the fight to take back our language."

Al chose leaders who understood the task and inspired excellence in their co-workers. "I thought it would take two election cycles before our message got out and convinced a large enough block of voters to gain recognition," I said. "But at the pace you're going, Al, we might be strong enough to field candidates from our movement on the ballot this coming Fall."

"But we have a serious problem," Al said.

"Yes?"

"Someone is leaking to Chief Alexander and Mayor Molson what we're up to."

"What makes you think that?" I asked.

"Our informant in the mayor's office reports that the mayor joked that we holy rollers enjoyed a sex orgy on the way to Joe's place on the river," Al said. "No one but the original eleven of us knew about our passing through the orgy on the way to Joe's house. Someone leaked that information.

"And it gets worse," Al said. "I agree with your suspicion that it is Joe, and he has overseen encrypting all our communication. So, he had access to all our phone calls and other files until I deleted them all last night."

Dread descended. I felt tightness in my chest, making it hard to breathe. *Oh no! Al erased all our plans, and ideas, and stories.* "Is any of the stuff you deleted saved in another folder?" I asked.

"All of it." Anger tainted Al's words. "Do you think I'm stupid?"

"Sorry, I was grossly underestimating you, Al. Please forgive me."

Al said nothing. It was as if his end of the phone line turned to stone, leaving me worrying for what seemed like forever. *Or maybe it's my tiny cell phone.*

Did it die? I wondered.

"The truth is," Al chuckled, "in my rush, I would have forgotten to save some files I was about to erase, if your wife hadn't pointed them out to me."

"The truth also is, I'm astounded by the excellence of your work, Al, down to the last painstaking detail." I paused to let my appreciation of Al sink in.

"Thanks," he said, voice quavering.

Knowing that 'getting emotional' was hard on Al, I changed the subject. "Now about spies in our group," I said, "do you suspect anyone besides Joe?"

"Not really," Al said. "And I find it hard to think of Joe as a traitor."

"Let's either keep any new plans to ourselves or feed him misinformation."

37. Solitary = Severe Seduction

Thursday, April 19

That night, in solitary confinement, the satanic music and seduction stopped. Five minutes later, Joe came to visit me. "Just wanted to know how you're doing."

"Okay." I shared the need to whisper when passing on 'classified' information (because the room might be bugged). By sharing this, I hoped to imply that I trusted him.

"Anything you need? Any messages you want to send through me?" Joe's questions fished for information that I was not going to be tricked into divulging.

"No," I said. "I'm sure they're doing their best to get me out of here as soon as possible," I said in a normal voice. Then in a whisper, I asked that the music piped into my room be classical or jazz.

"I heard that the chief thinks you are a risk for running away," Joe said, "so he has persuaded the judge to set the bail at five-hundred thousand dollars."

"Well, at last someone has recognized my value," I said aloud. "That malevolent devil," I whispered.

I don't remember what else we said. I was too astonished by the bail price to think of anything else. Shortly after Joe left, the seduction, counterbalanced by the angry rap, intensified.

I called my wife, told her what was going on, and asked her to pray aloud for me.

"Our loving heavenly Father," Kate prayed. "You wouldn't allow Dave to go through this unless you knew that with your help, he could pass the test. Help Dave to know these voices surrounding him are mere fantasy and their seductive words are lies. Remind him that as inviting as these women sound, they can't measure up to me, his wife. I am his only real flesh and blood lover. So, help him to keep choosing reality over fantasy. And help him to look forward to being in my arms that are aching to hold him.

"And, Father, rescue these women who are torturing my husband. Deliver them from the demons that torture them. And have mercy on the police chief and mayor. Forgive them, for they don't know what they're doing. Do this for Jesus' sake, who paid the ultimate price to rescue them from their folly. Amen."

I was stunned by Kate's merciful spirit toward those who were torturing me, especially the police chief and mayor. I didn't want them to be off the hook. But as I thought about it, I realized she was in line with God, who is not willing that any should perish, but that all should come to repentance.

A picture came to mind. I saw the mayor, the police chief, and me holding hands and looking up to Jesus on the cross. Each one of us was repenting of his sins as we heard Jesus say, "Father, forgive them because they didn't know what they were doing." I realized that I was not above, but on the same level as these wicked men. I needed His mercy as much as they did.

"Dave, are you still there?" Kate asked.

"Thank you, honey, for your loving words and tender, merciful attitude toward my enemies. When I get home, I'll tell you how it corrected my thinking. You will never know how much you've helped me in my quest to be like Jesus."

38. Thrown to the Wolves

Friday, April 20, 2018

Chief Alexander visited me the next morning. He asked how I liked having my private room with piped-in popular music and rousing messages.

"For what crime do I receive such a privilege?" I asked, every word oozing with satire.

The chief rattled off crimes he had already accused me of...."And what disturbs me personally is that a criminal like you dare speak disrespectfully of a representative of the law, calling me a malevolent devil."

All bogus or trumped-up charges. But he has proven that Joe can't be trusted. Only Joe heard me call Chief Alexander a malevolent devil, so Joe must have reported my foul language to Alexander.

"Oh, by the way, I've been re-reading your records," Alexander said. "This is not the first time you've interfered with police work. And in the process, you made enemies who happen to be locked up in this prison. Maybe I've been wrong to isolate you. You need exposure to your 'friends' here."

I grimaced but caught myself. "Whatever you think is best," I said, confronting him with what I felt was a look of stubborn resilience.

That afternoon a guard opened my cell door. "Go to the gym where everyone's watching the jail's top two teams fight for this year's championship," the guard said.

"I wondered what the noise was about. I'm not into noise. I'd rather go to the library," I said.

"What? You prefer books to championship basketball? Don't let that get out or you'll be the jail's wimp. Besides, attendance at group-building activities like this is mandatory."

"Do you and the other guards know that I was the detective who put together the facts that led to the imprisonment of at least six inmates here? Who knows how many of them are angry enough to risk spending more time in prison for the satisfaction of getting revenge?" Sweat ran down my face; my armpits were dripping as I imagined what I might have to face. "I can manage one or two at a time, but...."

A fight broke out on the other side of the gym. It was staged, I think, to pull attention away from the five guys approaching me. I recognized them as men I had helped incarcerate. *It looks like they knew I was coming. Who informed them? Joe?*

The first to approach...a tall skinny chap, I creatively labeled 'Number One.' *I locked him in a world without children because he molested children....*

"Take this," he grunted. He launched a knockout punch that I dodged, but just barely.

"Nice try, Buck." Number Two complimented his friend. Heavy, Number Two bounced around me like an eager boxer, itching to finish off his opponent. *You weren't so bouncy,* I recalled, *the day you got sent here for killing your wife with a brick that you claimed fell from a crumbling upper corner of your house.*

Bouncy tried to get behind me, but I defended my back-to-the-wall position with a kick that knocked him stumbling backward.

Punisher Number Three was tattooed, from the top of his bald head, down his thick neck and muscular arms to his skinny bared ankles. Before he could reach me with a slash or thrust, I launched a kick to his lower gut, causing him to double over, falling forward headfirst into the place I had just vacated...the gym's cinder block wall. His hard head hit something harder... hard enough to render him motionless.

The four fighters, still standing, seemed caught off guard by my fighting skills. They huddled together to plan their next approach. "We've been letting him fight one person at a time," Number One said. "He doesn't stand a chance against all four of us at once," said Number Two.

While they planned their next attack, I inched my way a few feet along the wall to a corner position, so that instead of being attacked from all four sides, I would have only two sides from which they could approach me. By then, the basketball champions were celebrating their narrow victory. In sports, there's the buildup to the final game with the winners celebrating and the losers feeling let down.

But today the losers' emotions ran high. Word spread excitedly that the newest inmate was a cop, a detective. "He's responsible for locking up six of us in this prison," Number One shouted. He used his height to point to the corner I had backed into. "Let the guys he put here be the ones who repay him," Number Two added.

Lord, I'm not getting outa' here alive, so I'm going to say what's on my heart: "Gentlemen, before you do whatever you do, I want you to know that the God who made you loves you even though you and I have rebelled against him. He sent his Son, Jesus, to forgive us rebels, and to live in us so that he can transform us to become like him."

While I talked Numbers One and Two and Four and Five formed a line hemming me in slightly outside striking distance. The crowd tightly surrounded the four fighters, so the guards couldn't penetrate the onlookers to stop the fight.

"We were just playing with you," Number Four claimed. "Now the fight begins. You're up against all of us at once."

For a few minutes, I held them off with kicks and punches. But they caught me off guard, toppling me to the floor where with fist or foot they unleashed their fury. I curled up in a protective posture. But they pulled my arms and legs straight, so they could kick and pummel me everywhere. The pain... stabbing, piercing, pounding, crushing... gave vent to their pent-up wrath against me and detectives in general.

I awoke in the prison clinic.

"How long have I been here?" I asked the nurse.

"Ten days," he said. "Long enough for us to find five fractured ribs, a green limb fracture of the lower left arm, a smashed nose, and a black eye which is much improved." He held a mirror up so I could see my left eye that, he told me, had been swollen shut. It offered just a slit to see through and was still colorful shades of purple, blending into yellow and green.

"Why is my throat so sore?" I asked.

"We used a feeding tube to feed you. It irritated your throat."

"And you kept me hydrated by this IV tube in my arm," I concluded.

"Yep. Took out the feeding tube when you started to wake up."

I tried to roll over but the pain in my rib cage and lower back shouted, "Don't move."

"Well, I guess I got off easy," I moaned. "Thank you, God."

"If I were you, I'd be mad at God for letting me get beat up so badly," the broad-shouldered nurse said.

"Why blame the One who protected me from worse damage...or death?" I asked. "Was it God who beat me up? If his laws had been respected, my enemies would have thanked me for enforcing them. By enforcing the law, I was punishing and correcting their demon-driven behavior. And by jailing them, I was preventing them from harming others. I'm always amazed at how people blame God for behavior fomented by Satan."

"What are you saying?" The nurse gave me a quizzical look.

"If we loved and obeyed God, our world would be only goodness— husbands and wives would be loving and faithful to one another; parents would nurture, love, and train their children in right living; employers would pay fair wages and see to the well-being of their employees; workers would do their best for their employers; governments would serve the people, not use them. But we gave up that goodness when we chose to do it our way, not God's way."

"Interesting." The nurse gave me a shot and scribbled some notes on the pad at the foot of the bed.

"Just as you keep notes on how I'm doing," I said, "God is keeping notes on how you're doing, you...." Drowsiness descended on me like a blanket of fog, making it difficult, but I said what I wanted to say, that is, "if you trust and love God and do as he teaches, God puts a smiling face on the pad...."

My eyelids closed. They were too heavy to open. But I could still hear. And what I heard I did not like.

"Keep him heavily sedated. He's dangerous!"

39. Escape from the Prison Clinic

April 30, 2018

Did my nurse forget to sedate me heavily enough? Or was it that change in meds? Or...Who knows? But I woke to the sound of the weather forecaster's voice on the radio. The clock on the wall told me it was the midnight news broadcast. The meteorologist signed off, making way for the anchor, who in a dismissive tone, was describing the formation of a new political party known as Pure Pleasure, whose goal would be to fight sex trafficking, especially prostitution and pornography.

As much as I wanted to stay glued to the radio, the chance to escape propelled me out of bed, sore as I was. The guard assigned to me was sound asleep in a chair to my left. To my right, stood two locked doors...the outer door let people from outside into a check-in area, through which you passed to get to the inner door that opened into a hallway leading to the clinic.

I found my clothes in a clear plastic bag under my bed. While I dressed, I heard Al Smith, chairperson of the Pure Pleasure Party, explain, "The political establishment will try to block Pure Pleasure from being on the ballot although we have a strongly developing following. If they succeed, we will conduct a write-in campaign that sends a message to the establishment. The people are saying, 'We're tired of your hollow promises, your profligate spending, your turning a blind eye to the sexual exploitation in our community, and your use of your office to serve yourselves, instead of working towards improvement for everyone.'"

Time ticked away as I pealed back the tape holding the lock picks deep in a fold under my arm. First, I selected a pick to release me from the ankle cuff. The guard interrupted his smooth snoring with a snort. *Oh, no, he's waking up.* But his soft, even breathing returned as I slipped a pick into the ankle cuff. It sprang open quickly, freeing me to get out of bed. I found my clothes in a plastic bag under my bed. I put them on over my prison clothes.

Seconds slipped by as I maneuvered the tiny but tough tools needed to break open the inner door lock. Each tick of the wall clock brought me closer to freedom or recapture. *Which would it be?* At last, the right tumblers fell, and I eased the door open and stepped into the check-in area.

The check-in area, staffed by an officer obsessed with his solitaire game, threatened to undo all the effort I had put into the escape. A four-foot-high counter stretched between the table where the guard played cards and the aisle that I had to use to get to the door. I kept my tall and painfully bruised body bent over to less than four feet high, so that the counter hid me, as I crept unseen past the guard. I continued to crouch as I picked the lock on the door to the outside. My shaky hands made the lockpicking extremely difficult.

Twenty seconds passed. Tick. Tick. Tick. Forty seconds. Tick. Tick. Tick. Sixty seconds. *I can't believe no one awakens. Uh, oh. Someone coming in from the outside... Do I hide and hope the person focuses forward while I slip out? Or do I stand tall, act as if I were an employee, pretend I'm looking for the right key while I let him unlock the door?* I fished through my picks, pretending I was looking for the key, and hoping the person now at the door didn't recognize me or suspect I was trying to escape.

I could have sworn the person coming from outside was sleepwalking. He unlocked and opened the door. We exchanged greetings. He went in and I went out into the night. In the Book of Acts, sleeping guards at two checkpoints allowed St. Peter to escape prison. *It looks like God's still in the jail-breaking business.*

40. Home at Last!

April 30, 2018

I took back streets on my walk home, ducking into shadows that hid me from being seen by passing motorists. Even so, I came close to being spotted when I was almost home. A squad car quit pursuing a speeding motorcyclist at the city border. The squad car turned around and with its searchlight began slowly examining my neighborhood. The searchlight almost caught me as I dashed to a bush between my house and my neighbor's. The cop must've seen my movement because he kept searching the bushes between the two houses with his spotlight. At last, he turned his light off, allowing me to finish crossing the space between our two houses.

Finally, I was home. Limping. Full of pain, but home. And that's all that mattered. I entered by the side door, which was hidden from snoopy neighbors by big bushes. The house, which had been trashed the day I had been jailed, was back to its pristine cleanliness and order.

That's my Kate; she brings order out of chaos. But how can I ease her into the disorder of seeing my battered body? Thank God, I have night's darkness to partially hide me during our first contact. I knocked lightly on the bedroom door while telling her in the romantic Spanish language that she was the only one: "Yo tengo esa costumbre de pensar en ti, cuando hablan de amor." (Translation: I have this habit of thinking of you when they talk about love.) To which Kate responded groggily, "Cada dia (every day)...."then realizing who was standing by the bed telling her he loved her, Kate leaped into my arms and whispered passionately "te quiero mas (I love you more)." Her tight hug hurt like hell, but healed like heaven's love, which was flooding my body and soul.

"Uh-oh," Kate released me. "You might be too sore for hugging. Sorry."

"Don't be. It hurt, but I needed it desperately. Just to be near you, to feel your presence. But I can't enjoy the luxury of being with you for very long. Having escaped from prison, I'm a wanted man. By now, they're searching for me."

"I wish I had a safe place where I could keep you near me," Kate said, as she pulled the curtains closed and turned on a lamp. She gasped. "What happened to your eye?"

"Five guys that I sent to prison welcomed me with their fists and karate kicks and I don't know what else. The nurse said I was unconscious ten days."

"Ten days?" tears flooded Kate's eyes. "You need specialists to oversee your recovery, honey. And we've got to find a lawyer who has the guts to defend you."

"Meanwhile, top priority is for me to stay hidden, and you can help with that by giving me one of your super disguises," I said. "Your disguise, together with my hair cut short, and beard gone, will enable me to walk around the city unrecognized.

Skillfully, Kate applied makeup that took attention away from the blackeye and made my face unrecognizable. As she created a new me, I sat beside her, holding her, massaging the tension out of her shoulders.

"I will call you the first chance I get," I promised.

"I trust you to do what's best," she said as she grabbed a spray can left over from a costume party two months earlier, she put gray streaks in my hair, making me look twenty years older.

"Look at you," Kate said. "Hunched shoulders, a wrinkled face, gray hair...and...." she took down a cane from a hook in the side doorway and put it in my hands. "Now hobble out of here old man, before they catch you."

As she pushed me out the door, she planted a kiss squarely on my lips. Her kiss conveyed more than words the desire to be together, creating in me the dream of pure pleasure.

#

I climbed the hill behind our neighborhood and had reached the crest when I heard sirens. I looked down to see two police cars stopping at my house.

Officers from one car ran and scaled the fence even though, if they had checked, the gate was unlocked. They ran to the back of the house to cut off any escape via the backyard, I assumed. Finding none, they began probing the neighbors' high bushes and hedges.

Meanwhile, the two officers from the other car knocked on the front door, first lightly, then more and more loudly. I knew Kate was putting off opening the door to give me more time to get away. She also had to be sure Marta, Krystyl, and Heather, were hidden in their assigned places in the attic, but our delay came at a cost to our neighbors. As I watched houses light up and heard children calling in fearful voices to their parents, I became increasingly upset. *Thanks, guys, for waking all my neighbors.*

They're going to love me for this. But this isn't the time to make things right with the neighbors. I've got to find a hiding place before dawn.

On the other side of the hill that ascended from our backyard, stood the church that our family attended. The pastor's house was on the same campus. I descended to the church campus, picked the lock on the garage door, entered, locked the door behind me, and collapsed into sleep on the rear seat of the pastor's soon-to-be-retired Chevrolet Classic.

41. Abolition of Sexploitation

May 1, 2018

I woke to the shake, rattle, and roll of the old Chevrolet thrumming to life. The engine was sluggish, so, Pastor Tony let it idle. *Do I run the risk of scaring him? Why not? Better to do it now than when he's out in traffic.* I sat up like a jack-in-the-box.

He jumped, head hitting the ceiling, and straight-arming the horn which chimed the opening notes of *Amazing Grace*. I couldn't hold back a burst of laughter, despite the tsunami of pain that swept across my body due to my sudden movement.

"Pastor Tony, I'm Dave Von Moeller. As you see, I'm disguised...."

He turned and shook my hand. "Boy, you scared me to death," he said with an expression halfway between 'don't you ever try that again' and 'well done.' "Speaking of fear and death, we were afraid you were killed in that infamous prison, when we didn't hear from you for so many days. I can't put in words how good it is to see you, although you've aged remarkably in the last several weeks."

"I escaped last night, went home long enough for Kate to disguise me, and chose to hide in your garage because the cops were scouring my neighborhood. May I hide out here for a few days? I could use some rest."

"There's a good hiding place in the church basement. I'll show you where it is...once we set a time for you to meet with major creators of the PPP, you know, the Pure Pleasure Party."

"I know."

"Of course, but what you don't know is what we've accomplished while you were in prison. I was just about to meet up with people inspired by our vision. Would you like me to bring them to the church, so we can bring you up to speed?"

"That would be great!" I couldn't stifle a yawn.

"Let's get you to that hiding place, so you can rest, " Pastor Tony said. "I will postpone the meeting until later this evening."

#

That evening Pastor Tony awakened me and took me upstairs where the smell of coffee wafted through the hall. I easily detected my wife's voice out of all the chattering. *Oh, to be with her!*...and the others again. I wanted to rush to embrace Kate but my battered body refused to move any faster than the old man I was disguised to be. Walking with the aid of the cane, I approached the door .

I had arranged through Pastor Tony, to let Kate introduce me so we could tell if they would know me in my disguise. And that's what Kate did in her own inimitable way. She ran to greet this totally strange old man. With her arm around my arm, she asked them, "Do any of you know this gentleman?" The people in the room included Marta, Krystyl, and Heather. Al, Pete, and Ron were also part of the gathering. No one knew who the old man was.

"I'm surprised," Kate faked a puzzled look. "Krystyl and Marta, don't tell me you don't know a man who helped you escape a mansion fire, found part of the Underground Railway with you, and went on a canoe trip with you?"

"You seem to be talking about Dad." Jenna said, "But this man is not Dad."

"How do you know?" Kate asked.

"Look at him. He's not at all like Dad."

"Okay. We can't recognize him if we go by looks. Are looks the only way we can recognize someone?"

"Can he talk to us?" Marta asked.

"Sure, go ahead and let us hear your voice, Sir," Kate said.

"I never thought you, my friends and family, would force me to verify who I am," I complained jokingly.

As I spoke, a hush came over the group. Then came a muttering of "isn't he in prison?" and "prison couldn't have aged him that much" and "that old-timer sure is a good mimicker."

Kate cleared up the confusion everyone was feeling. "Thanks for assuring me my disguise worked. Yes, this is my husband, Dave Von Moeller."

"Amazing!" Jenna said. "You don't look at all like Dad."

"That's for sure," Heather said.

"Just now I realized that unmasking disguises, is part of our job," Pastor Tony said.

"Right!" I said. "We want to expose our city leaders who disguise visiting a prostitute or viewing porn as sexual freedoms. The truth is those 'freedoms' are bondage for both the victim and the abuser."

"Now, to change the subject, I've heard bits and pieces about this new political party. Could you give me more details?" I asked.

"As an organizer, Al has been amazing," Kate said. "He's bringing together community leaders whom he knows well from his years as a neighborhood watch organizer for the police force."

"Then, Pete is bringing together even more community leaders in our city and county," Al joined in. "During his years as captain of the Fire Department he formed strong bonds between himself and these leaders."

"And I am contacting pastors and youth leaders of churches citywide," Ron said. " I have more time on my hands now since I was forced to retire."

"We've started gathering people in homes and neighborhood groups, churches and town halls to show them the reality of sexual exploitation. I think we're all shocked by how deeply entrenched and devastating it is," Kate said. "What scares me the most is the way it has spread amongst our children. Five short blocks from the city's premier middle school, an adult sex shop reaches out to middle schoolers via outdoor displays on stands that can be swept inside in a few seconds in the unlikely event that an inspector was to come along."

"Just two blocks from the largest city high school they've planted a very alluring adult sex store," Heather said. "I know, because I checked it out and found it to have too much of a pull on me, so I quit going."

"You're smart to let no one control you but you," Marta said.

"But Kate and Dave, you tell us we should surrender control of our lives to Jesus!" Krystyl appeared to be stymied.

"True," Kate smiled, realizing how confusing we could be. "Just look at yourself. Don't you have more control over yourself now than you did a month ago? Are you doing drugs? No! Stealing? No! Complaining? Well, maybe a little; Quarrelling? No! Bursting with anger? No! Nursing revenge? No! Only a month ago, you were the victim of all these things. Your former life was out of control. But now you are gaining freedom from these things. Do you think Jesus might have something to do with that? The fact is, the more you yield control to Jesus, the more self-control you have."

Jumping in, I added, "Many West Wenders would tell you, 'I'm in control of my life. Nobody tells me what to do, thank you.' But they're actually under the control of people like the mayor and police chief, or creditors who they're afraid to offend. Or...." Noticing nodding heads and droopy eyes, I got their attention by asking them to name things that subtly or blatantly control people. They called out:

"Pride,"	"Lust,"	"Boasting,"
"Greed,"	"Gluttony,"	"Bitterness,"
"Envy,"	"Laziness,"	"Anger."

"All of these things that control people could lead to sexual exploitation," I said. "Take bitterness, for example. If life has been hard, it is natural to complain. You can easily take it a step further and become bitter. As a bitter person you'll gravitate toward others who, like you, focus on their pain or loss, and feel they have a right to feel sorry for themselves because life has been so unfair. As an escape from their misery, some bitter people turn to illicit sex. Being totally focused on their own pain, they have no regard for the person they're sexually exploiting and abusing."

"Of the things we have listed, lust seems the most obvious precursor to sexual exploitation," Kate said. "If left unchecked, its appetite grows monstrously, often including exploitive sexual behavior."

"Our culture idolizes sex which makes it more likely that people characterized by the list we made will use sex wrongly—to fix themselves, or prove themselves, or relieve themselves," I said.

"Those are selfish uses of sex," Kate said. "Pure sex is unselfish. It doesn't take, it gives. Your highest pleasure comes from pleasing the one you love."

"Pure sex is rooted in perfect love. Perfect love is loving just as Jesus loved," I said. "Not some imagined Jesus who is there to satisfy your selfish desires but the real Jesus you find in the Bible. How did he love? Can we love like that? No way!"

"But as we get to know Jesus, seeing his faithfulness and experiencing his love, we find it safe to put our trust in him and surrender control of our lives to him," said Pastor Tony.

"Can you love the people in your daily lives the way Jesus loves them?" Ron asked. "That's what we are beginning to see happen as everyone in the Pure Pleasure Party learns and carries out his role in the Big Three with excellence."

"Big Three?" I queried.

"Everyone needs to have a significant role to play if a movement or a political party is to be successful," Ron said. "We are going to do this by giving to every member a significant do-able task to carry out according to his availability, abilities, and interests. Each task furthers the mission of the Pure Pleasure Party, which asks members, surrendered to Christ's will, to:

One. Discover, i.e., get to know all that is happening in the sex trade in our city and county. This knowledge will come from interviewing current and former prostitutes and other sex trade workers; via examining what's being done to help victims by government, church, and other agencies; via (where possible) observing and conversing with people profiting from the sex trade.

Two. Filter via gathering into useable categories the facts, statistics, and questions/topics uncovered in the Discover phase; rigorously checking assertions to determine their truthfulness; placing assertions into these categories: a. truth, b. perspective of interviewee, c. viewpoint of writer/reporter, d. reasonable conclusion, e. mere speculation, f. lies.

Three. Tell compelling stories that show the sufferings of people trapped in the sex trade, portraying the dangers, failings, and the slow paths to success for people in recovery, using information from phases one and two in articles, podcasts, human interest stories, interviews, and other forms of messaging. The possibilities are endless," Ron said.

"People are eager to participate in transforming the city once they see how it can be done and what role they play." Kate said. "These people form the backbone of our 'hoped-for' political party."

Overwhelmed by the daunting nature of what we faced, I suggested we commit our plans and concerns to our Father, who cared, more deeply than we, about this evil in our community.

42. I Fire My Lawyer

I tried my best to keep from belching the sour squirt of stomach acid burning my esophagus as I glanced around my lawyer's office and thought of how little he had done for me. But Kate's earnest prayer for my tormentors convicted me. So begrudgingly, I asked God to help me act lovingly toward him.

"I shouldn't be seeing you here in my office," the lawyer said as I stood facing him across from his desk. *He didn't even invite me to sit.*

"Because...?" I questioned.

"Because you should be in jail for breaking out of jail," he said. "I could be caught harboring a fugitive from justice."

"Are you serious?" I said, pointing to my disguised face. "You couldn't recognize me. I told you my own daughter couldn't recognize me. This disguise is my gift to you so that no one will ever know I visited you unless you tell them. I did this for you, what have you done for me?"

"You know the procedure here. Everything has to go through the big bosses. If they don't like what you propose they have ways of squelching not only your proposal, but you."

"I know, but did you at least try?" My lawyer squirmed uncomfortably in his seat. "You should've gotten me out of jail the very first day. You know solitary confinement is applied to prisoners who are the worst of the worst. You knew my so-called crimes did not merit setting bail at half a million dollars.

On those grounds alone, you could have freed me from prison, or at least placed me with inmates who would've been safe to live with.

"You knew they put me in with the general population where six people had it in for me because my detective work put them in prison. You must have heard that five of them jumped me and beat me within an inch of my life. I was ten days in a coma. Did you wish I would die, so the problem of working with me would be solved? I could have been spared all this if you had done your job. Not once did you contact me. Where were you?"

"I'm sorry," he said, without conveying any sense of regret.

"Sorry?" I asked. "Is that all? How about an explanation? Where were you?"

"That's privileged information."

"Since it almost cost me my life, and since I'm paying you to help me deal with these criminals, shouldn't I have the privilege of knowing what's going on?"

"You can't imagine the pressure they put on me."

"Does 'they' include Chief Alexander and Mayor Molson?" I asked.

He didn't answer, his face was a mask. But he was biting his lower lip as if nervously holding something in. "I'll have to get another lawyer since you're afraid to defend me," I said.

"That's fine with me," he said. "But I'm telling you, you won't find another lawyer in this county willing to have anything to do with this case."

"Then I'll go outside of the county." Remembering that I had prayed to love my enemy, I shook his hand. I looked him in the eyes and predicted, "There's coming a day when you will realize that as long as we let fear rule this county, innocent people will get hurt because the path to justice will be barred."

43. Justice at Last!

As soon as I left his office, I contacted Alliance Defending Freedom, an international non-profit legal aid agency. They assured me that they would find a nearby lawyer to defend me. When I met their lawyer, later that week, I gasped. *How can someone so young have the maturity needed for our case? Plus, given his swarthy features, I doubt that my community will view him with respect.*

But I discovered that my lawyer, Bashir Ahmad, a Middle Eastern man in his mid-twenties, with dark, neatly combed hair, was more qualified than I imagined. He came from a neighboring county run by corrupt officials like ours. Familiar with the legal landscape (or shall we say the illegal terrain) of our county, he nodded with understanding as I explained our situation.

"Given the kind of people in power," he said, "it doesn't matter how serious the charges or how convincing our case. It doesn't matter how believable our witnesses are, if the jurors fear reprisal from the police chief and mayor, then we don't stand a chance. You might think things will go easy on you, since you've been left alone and not put back in jail, but that's only because they don't want to compromise their public image right now. The dirty duo, as you have sometimes called them," he said, adding air quotes with his finger, " have perfected the art of creating fear and loyalty through severe punishment."

"Add to that the 'insult' of the defense team stooping so low as to hire an Arab to represent them against the testimony of two sterling white police officers, who are 'local boys.'" Bashir laughed at his self-deprecating humor, and I joined him in hearty guffaws. "It will take a miracle to win this," Bashir admitted, his countenance clouding momentarily.

"But if no one dares stand up against evil because everyone thinks it's impossible to defeat, then it will be impossible to defeat," I stated.

"Besides, even if we lose the trial," Bashir said, "the trial itself will pull back the curtain that hides and protects the gross cruelty of sexual exploitation in this community."

"Exactly!" I gave him the thumbs up signal. *He understands what we are up against, and yet is still willing! Amazing! Maybe we got us the right lawyer after all.*

#

Bashir requested a preliminary hearing in which each side laid out all the evidence they planned to use to prove their opponent was wrong and they were right.

The prosecuting attorney faced the judge and said, "Mr. Von Moeller is being charged with endangerment of a child." He then gave an expanded list of my misdeeds.

Bashir responded, "The prosecution accuses Mr. Von Moeller of putting Heather through all these dangers which would be cruel, if not unlawful, if there had been a safer way to escape those who pursued them and held them captive. I hope the witnesses on my client's behalf show that his heart was set, not on putting Heather in dangerous situations, but on saving Heather from real danger."

Bashir's witnesses, especially Heather, described me as being a co-victim of some of these dangers, and rescuer from other dangers, and never was I a perpetrator.

But more importantly, Bashir showed that her stepfather's cruelty to her was so frequent and damaging that the courts had emancipated her, which meant she was legally an adult. And because she was an adult legally all those bogus child endangerment charges didn't apply. To my amazement, Bashir convinced the judge that there was not enough evidence to bring the case against me to trial.

I was free! Here I had rigorously prepared for intense warfare. I feared yet looked forward to fighting the invincible powers that governed and guarded our city. I felt let down. The judge judged according to the law, not according to 'the way we always do it,' the 'we' being made up of the mayor, police chief and their cronies.

I felt deflated rather than elated. I had imagined myself as having a larger role, more to do, therefore a greater significance. My sense of loss came from missing the satisfaction that comes with a hard-earned victory. To have it finished by a preliminary hearing in less than three hours, diminished our work. It was too easy. *How dare I think like this? We asked for God's help. If he makes it easy for us, can't we accept it?*

44. Memory of Justice

Word of our victory over the mayor and police chief spread rapidly through the ranks of the Pure Pleasure Party. So also did the accounts of my cruel imprisonment, and my escape from the prison clinic. Pure Pleasure Partiers spread these stories to their friends, neighbors, relatives, and various media.

Our contact in the mayor's office told us that the mayor and the police chief, seeing that the public was turning against them, decided to back off from harassing us, hoping that would win favor. They thought it best to be conciliatory, to which I responded with a note to the press thanking the mayor and police chief for their kindness to me.

We didn't realize the extreme weight we had been carrying until it was lifted. I hummed gospel tunes, walked in the woods, began reading *Mere Christianity*, an excellent explanation of Jesus and his church. I hoped it would prepare me to represent Jesus and his way in our fight against sexual exploitation.

And Kate? Along with her flock — Marta, Krystyl, Heather, Jenna, and sometimes me— she, with us, created fabulous meals, made quilts, knitted sweaters or small things like mittens and baby booties, played piano, sang hymns and other uplifting songs. Best of all, Kate snuggled close beside me as we each read from our favorite authors.

Jenna and Heather enjoyed competing at chess and hiking with Krystyl, Marta, Kate, and me in a nearby state park.

We visited five rehabs with Krystyl and Marta. The Adult and Teen Challenge Center fifty miles south of town exceeded our expectations. The curriculum covered overcoming drugs, sexual addiction, and other addictions. I saw a section on shame and other results of abuse, which I thought would really be helpful.

The girls chatted excitedly on the ride home, "The staff and students warmly welcomed us," Marta said.

"Let's enroll soon," Krystyl said, as they arrived home. "They said we could come as early as next week."

"Sounds good to me," Marta replied.

As the girls settled into a game of chess, Kate sighed a breath of relief. "I can't believe how well everything is working out."

Knock. Knock. Knock.

"It's the police," I said as I looked out the window. "How can we help you?" I asked, as Krystyl and Marta looked up from the chessboard.

"We're here to question Ms. Krystyl Li and Ms. Marta Rodriguez about the murder of Ms. Ana Mills."

"Murder? Ms. Mills committed suicide," I protested, and planted my feet to prevent the police from getting any further into our living room.

"Not so!" the police spokesperson said. "We have reason to believe it was a homicide. We're here to take these girls down to the Public Safety Building (PSB) for questioning. So, Ms. Li and Ms. Rodriguez need to come with me."

"You haven't shown us your credentials or the summons for these two women," I protested.

The police officer thumbed through papers he retrieved from his vest pocket and showed them to me. Satisfied, I said I'd follow them down to the PSB and go in to observe the questioning. But when we got there, two hefty guards blocked my way, mocking my protests.

#

Remembering the tortures inflicted on me when I was a resident in the so-called Public *Safety?* Building, I was hounded by worry for Marta and Krystyl. It helped when Kate, Jenna, and Heather joined me in asking God to keep them safe and inspire them to tell their cellmates the positive changes their new friend, Jesus, was making in their lives.

Bashir Ahmad agreed to represent them, for which I was grateful. During the trial, to play it safe, and to eliminate hotel expenses, Bashir stayed with us.

On Bashir's fourth night with us, we had finished dinner and were relaxing in our living room. While reading the Bible together, we came to the fifth chapter of James who counsels us to confess our faults one to another and pray for one another. "Let me get my fault off my chest," I told Bashir. "I was scared of you on two counts when you were chosen to represent me."

"Was it because of my Arabic name?"

Hanging my head, I nodded.

Bashir reached over and playfully punched my shoulder. "People think that having an Arabic-sounding name means you must be Muslim. Not so. Many Christians in the Middle East have Arabic names, including me and my family. And there are people of other religions, besides Muslim and Christian, who speak Arabic and have Arabic names.

"Some Middle Easterners think having an Arabic name provides the protection of sameness. They fit right in. But having an Arabic name does not guarantee safety. Many Arabic Christians are being driven out of their homes. They are beaten severely, raped, and starved in refugee camps. Yes, we have experienced what your family has gone through— wrongful imprisonment, being hunted down, horrible beatings, murder...

"What was the other thing about me that scared you?" Bashir asked.

"Your youth. You look like a college student. So, I doubted that you had the experience needed...."

"I cut my teeth in a legal system like yours, but far worse. My dad was a lawyer. He and I discussed his cases, and with the help of knowledge my dad gave me, I finished law school at age twenty-two. Since then, I have fought many legal battles in my homeland where the most powerful people make all the rules and the weak have no hope of justice. I'd far rather work here. People in this land at least have a memory of fairness, justice, and truth to which we can appeal."

45. Everyone Loves a Good Story

To counter the prosecuting attorney's boasting that he would prove Ana Grimes was thrown into the river by her treacherous, so-called friends, defense attorney, Bashir Ahmad challenged the jury to think. Bashir asked, "Who are you most likely to believe–a police officer whose job is to protect you and your community or a prostitute whose job wreaks havoc on our communities? It would be right to favor the cop over the prostitute in many cases. But can you, with an open mind, seek to discern who is telling the truth in this case? Is it the cops or the prostitutes?" Bashir sought the eyes of each juror as he asked the question again. "Can you discern who is truthful?... I think you can."

#

Testifying for the prosecution, Charlie Jacobs, one of two officers at the scene, described how the girls hit each other with their paddles. "They shouted at each other. When we called them to shore... That's when one of them stood and the other two pushed her out of the canoe."

"Could their hitting each other with paddles be due to their simply being clumsy at managing a canoe?" Bashir asked.

"It's possible," Charley admitted.

"According to your description, Ana stood up in the canoe. When do people stand in a canoe?" Bashir asked Charley.

"When they are getting in or out," Charley answered.

"How far was the canoe from the shore?" Bashir asked.

"Twenty or thirty feet."

" Too far out for disembarking, right?" Bashir asked.

"Right," Charley said. "Where she jumped out, she was in over her head." Realizing his slip, Charley clapped his hands over his mouth, only partly hiding the deepening redness of his face.

"She jumped?" The pitch of Bashir's voice climbed an octave.

"No! I didn't mean that. I meant to say where they pushed her out."

"You have a right to change your story," Bashir said graciously. "Just keep in mind that each change makes your story less believable."

"Your Honor, he's... mocking the witness," the prosecuting attorney complained.

"I'd hardly call it mocking," the Judge commented. "But" turning now to Bashir, he said, "Your worthy opponent may rightly object to your advising his client concerning the believability of his testimony. Now please continue."

"Charley, you said you saw one of them stand up, and then the other two pushed her out. If the girls had wanted to drown her, wouldn't they be making the first move, by pulling her from a sitting position to at least part way standing so they could shove her out? But you said, you saw Ana stand up first."

"...Yes." Charley hesitated.

"Could the fact that she stood up first, tell us that this was her choice? While we may never know her reasons, is it possible that she intended to jump?"

Charley shrugged.

"Is it also possible that what you saw as pushing, was Krystyl and Marta actually trying to prevent her from jumping?"

"I guess." Charley mumbled.

"You said they were shouting at each other. What exactly were they saying?"

Charley wiped sweat from around his collar. "All three were talking at once, so I couldn't catch what they said," Charley responded.

"So, you don't know what Ana said or did that would make both of her friends want to murder her. Without any discussion, you're saying, not just one, but both decided to kill her.

"They murdered their friend right in front of the police, despite knowing that this would land them in prison, possibly for life. I wonder if anyone finds that hard to believe?" Bashir looked at the jurors. As Charley left, Bashir called Marta to the witness stand. "Now, let me introduce you to one of Ana's so-called murderers."

#

Some of us, observing the trial, wept as Bashir tenderly helped Marta describe the dark void she descended into when her mother sold her to the smartly dressed lady. We stood on tiptoe with then three-year old Marta while she stretched to see out the back window of a cab, trying to capture one final glimpse of her mother. Our hearts jumped when she screamed, 'Mama! Mama! Mama!' Begging her mother to come and rescue her. But the last image she had of her mother was her shrinking into the distance.

Bashir led us to the cow shed where Marta and thirty or more other captured girls ate and slept, defecated, and urinated, fought and co-existed. We saw her eyes widen, her mouth drop open, then close too late, when an angry guard splashed a bucket of feces and urine in her face. We soaked in the stench of her humiliation.

The prosecuting lawyer objected, breaking the spell. "Irrelevant, Your Honor."

"Your Honor, these women are on trial for murder. If we send them up for life, it's only fair to at least know who they are," Bashir said.

"Objection overruled," the judge stated emphatically.

Bashir has the judge chomping at the bits to hear the rest of the story, I smiled. *Maybe we have a chance after all.*

"So, what happened next?" Bashir asked Marta.

"The guard ripped off my dress and told me to use it to clean up the mess."

"Marta, go back to that stinking cow shed, as an adult. What did that three-year old girl feel?"

"I feel shame. Someone had stolen my underwear. I stood there naked and alone with all eyes on me. The adult me, wants to rip that guard's clothes off in a very public place, and let her feel what it's like to be caught naked. The child me stiffens. I can't move. I don't know what to do."

"Were there other punishments you received while growing up?"

"Many."

"Why didn't you run away?"

"When we were little, our owners frightened us with horrible stories of what it was like outside. And the brave ones who did run away, the owners always caught and beat, sometimes with thorned branches until blood covered their bodies."

"So, you were imprisoned by fear," Bashir said.

"Or hooked by 'love' or drugs," Marta said.

"What does hooked by 'love' mean?" Bashir asked Marta.

"When we were children, some of us tried to be our guard's favorite, because favorites got more love, that is, more privileges and special treats. The few of us who survived into adulthood, fought to be our pimp's favorite. He might beat us at times, but he gave us privileges others didn't get."

"Your honor, we fail to see the relevance of these sob stories." The prosecuting lawyer stood, stomping, and making a show of looking at his watch.

"Continue." The judge nodded his head toward Bashir, who kindly dismissed Marta and brought Krystyl to the stand.

"Why did pimps play favorites, Krystyl?" Bashir asked.

"Their ultimate goal was to make us submissive," Krystyl said. "They cultivated my natural desire to please my superiors by giving me nicer clothing, more food, and better jobs. Then they goaded the other children, telling them, ' If you were more like Krystyl, we would love you like we love her.' You can imagine how popular that made me. But I'd rather put up with the kids' scorn than to lose the owners' favor."

"So, you stayed with your owners out of submissive loyalty and fear?" Bashir stroked his chin, and looked toward the jury, expressing puzzlement. "But for some reason this time your fearful loyalty was not strong enough to prevent you from trying to escape from your pimps or whoever your owners were."

"This time the police, that is, the corrupt ones, were hot on our trail because we knew too much about their involvement in sex trafficking. It's a long story, involving corrupt police protecting the sex trade against people, including good cops, trying to stop this abusive form of slavery, from which we were rescued. Marta and I and Ana joined the anti-sex slavery movement, when we realized that there was a better way."

Bashir paused, looked down at his papers as if gathering his thoughts.

"May I add one more reason why we are no longer controlled by pimps or the fear of other evil men?" Krystyl asked.

"Feel free," Bashir said.

"After being abused for so many years, it's hard to not feel wasted, ruined, and good for nothing but prostitution," Krystyl said. "Good for nothing! That's the lie Satan wants me to believe about myself. On the other hand, if we trust in what Jesus has done for us, including his lovingly adopting us into God's family, God assures Marta and me that he will watch over us like a loving parent, and place us where we can best work together with him. Right now, he has given us the honor of living in the jail where we enjoy the privilege of demonstrating the truth about our heavenly Fa...."

"Your honor, could we cut out all this religious stuff?" the prosecuting attorney interrupted explosively.

"This 'religious stuff', as you know, your honor, is the foundation of our laws. It upholds all that is decent and orderly," Bashir calmly addressed the judge. "It's the religious stuff that raised Krystyl from the gloomy depths of thinking she was worthless to the heights of her being a mentor, providing helpful companionship and wise counsel to jailed inmates."

"Objection overruled," the judge intoned. "Please continue, Mr. Ahmad."

Bashir Ahmad took a long deep breath, "One last question, Krystyl. Were you abused by someone in this room?" Bashir extended his arms to include all the people gathered in this hall of judgment....

"Objection!" The prosecutor bellowed. "The defense is attempting to put the whole audience on trial, as if they were defendants. If our courts allowed such reckless manipulations, our legal system would be in shambles."

The judge looked at his watch. "It's noon. The court is in recess until 1:30," he said.

"Follow me", the judge said to the attorneys for defense and prosecution. Hardly had they entered the judge's chambers when the judge turned to Bashir and asked, "What are you trying to do?"

"I have no intention of pushing anyone to divulge that he has been to a prostitute," Bashir said. "I only wish to help people see what it's like for Krystyl and Marta to live under a cloud of suspicion."

"And how do you propose to do that?" the prosecuting attorney asked.

"By putting both Marta and Krystal on the witness stand and then saying to everyone: I don't want anyone to say anything, just look at these two women and try to imagine what it would be like to be in their shoes. They were deceptively ripped from their families in early childhood; never went to school; used virtually all their lives in the sex trade; despised by most people, lived under a cloud of suspicion, yet still able to laugh, to see and delight in the richly colored floral wonders of this season of summer; able to trust God and to care for hurting people. I hope to win well-deserved sympathy, if not admiration, for Marta and Krystyl by reviewing these facts," Bashir said.

"I concede that you can bewitch some with your soft sell. But you won't get them all. I can read a jury. I've got at least three whom you haven't won over with your silver tongue," the prosecutor boasted. "And I only need one to hang the jury."

"And I concede that you have a better chance of achieving a hung jury, than we have of completely exonerating the women," Bashir said. "But it won't be the power of bewitching that clears their names. It will be the power of truth."

"If you two have finished, I'd like to get on with my lunch." The judge held the door for the two lawyers. "See you at 1:30," he said.

#

We used the rest of the lunch time to plan our strategy for the afternoon session. On the previous evening, we had experienced an unusual sense of God's presence during a phone conversation with Krystyl and Marta, who were out on bail and staying with Pastor Tony's family It was as if we were all in one room together with the Lord.

"I want you to recall that amazing awareness of God being with us last night," Pastor Tony said. "What did it mean to you, Krystyl, and to you, Marta?"

"I had an overwhelming sense of being cleansed and made pure," Krystyl said.

"Me, too," Marta said. "I recalled the hard scrubbing the smartly dressed lady made me endure after taking me out of the filthy cow shed. That was nothing compared to the scrubbing I enjoyed last night. And I stood under a mighty waterfall to rinse off the soap."

"Do you find in your heart any traces of guilt and shame?" Bashir asked.

All of us—Krystyl, Marta, Ron, Bashir, Al, Heather, Jenna, Kate, Pete, Pastor Tony, and I—had been in on last night's conversation with Jesus. And we all searched our hearts. We reported similar experiences captured in words such as, "the shame, so deeply embedded, is totally uprooted" or "I'm free from its oppressive weight."

"Why do you think God visited us in that incredible way?" I asked.

"To boost our faith in a time when it's hard to believe God is at work," Kate said.

"To give us the comfort of knowing that God is here with us." Ron said.

"Think about the message He gave us. Who else needs that message?" I asked.

"The mayor," someone said. "The police chief," "the corrupt cops," "the pimps," "the prostitutes, who although they are forced against their will to do what they do, they bear oppressive shame."

"Even though I know that God wants to forgive them, what if I don't want to see a certain person forgiven?" Marta asked. "I've had some johns who are so perverted that the only place they'd feel at home would be hell ."

"That's kind of the way I felt about Boris," Jenna said. "I couldn't imagine a pervert like him in heaven. But now, I can't imagine heaven without him."

"How do we communicate that message of radical love and forgiveness?" Heather asked.

"With the powerful hand of God," Bashir said. "He wants us to trust him for something big, a God-sized miracle. Let's not insult him by expecting defeat. Now let's review our plan for our time at court this afternoon," Bashir said. "At a certain time, I'll call Krystyl and Marta to the witness stand. Then I will ask everyone to contemplate about what it would be like to be in your shoes, Marta, and Krystyl. During that time, I want you two to count how many users of your services you see in the room. Try to make eye contact with them and silently, tell them with your eyes that in Jesus' name you forgive them. Can you do that?

"Gladly. I want the entire world to experience the lavish forgiveness God has given me," Krystyl said.

"I can't do it." Marta stared at the floor, her hands folded and pushing hard upwards under her chin. "I can't lie or fake it. If I see certain men, I won't be communicating forgiveness with my eyes, but disgust and hatred."

"Thank you for your honesty, Marta.," Kate said. "I have been struggling with fear that if I see them, I will despise and hate the men who almost killed Dave while he was in prison. I've mentally said 'yes' to their being forgiven. And it helps to know Dave has forgiven them. But I don't know if I could shake the hands that beat my husband to oblivion."

"Forgiveness is too difficult a work to do on our own. We need Jesus, the Supreme Forgiver to do that work in us," Pastor Tony said. "He's dwelling in us. Somehow, we need to let him be his forgiving self, in and through us."

"Years ago, my wife was held at gunpoint... and raped." pastor Tony seemed to be struggling as he began telling his story. "I knew God wanted me to forgive the man, but I couldn't. What I mean is that I didn't feel like forgiving him. I wanted to take a chainsaw and cut off his arms and legs and the apparatus between his legs and let him bleed out. I know this is gross, but I want you to know the rage I felt. How could I ever forgive him? But God's Spirit was persistent. 'Forgive him, as I have forgiven you,' he kept whispering in my ear.

Then God gave me a picture of myself and that man standing beneath Jesus at the cross. I got the message. I needed the forgiveness provided by Jesus as much as that cruel man needed it. The picture changed and I saw myself taking the rapist by the hand to Jesus. I agreed, in my mind, if not yet in my feelings, with Jesus' desire to rescue that man from his evil ways."

"I know you wish I could forgive even if I don't feel it, but I can't," Marta said. "I feel like I would be lying."

"You are experiencing one of the important ways that Jesus leads us, which is to follow your conscience. I am sorry for pressuring you to go against it," Bashir said. "Are you up for at least counting the men, in the court room, who have used your services?"

"Yeah, I can do that," Marta said.

Bashir looked at his watch, and said, "It's late; no time for prayer but as we go back to court, let's be prayerfully expecting a miracle."

#

The moment came in the afternoon session when Bashir called Marta and Krystyl to the witness stand. "I know that calling more than one witness at a time is unusual, but the judge has given me permission. I am asking everyone in the jury to think about these two women and all that they've been through."

Directing his face towards the women, he said, "I asked, in this morning's session, if either of you were abused by anyone in this room."

Then facing the court room spectators and jury, Bashir said, "I don't know if I'm going to have Marta and Krystyl point out who you are, but if you have used their services, they know who you are, and they have been counting how many of their clients are here."

The crowd shifted uneasily, some crossing or uncrossing their legs, some clearing their throats or glancing around the room. Of those who glanced, their eyes came to rest on the police chief and the mayor. It was a commonly held assumption that West Wend's leaders were getting rich from their protecting the illegal sex trade.

"Krystyl and Marta," Bashir said, "I know you can't see everywhere, but from where you are, tell us how many of your former clients you've seen in this room."

"Seven," Krystyl responded.

"Nine," Marta said.

"Sixteen, out of a capacity crowd of one hundred." Bashir ran his fingers through his hair. "Wouldn't knowing there's that many johns amongst you cast the dark shadow of mistrust over you all, making it hard to do business or form relationships? That shadow has hovered over Marta and Krystyl almost all their lives. Who's going to trust a prostitute?"

"Objection!!" yelled the prosecutor. " We are getting into pure speculation."

"Objection sustained," said the judge.

"Your honor, I was simply trying to help the jury understand what it is like to be under a cloud of suspicion, as Marta and Krystyl have been." Bashir said.

His face red with fury, the mayor pounded his fist on the table to accent his outrage. "Why are so many of you people looking at me?" he asked the room full of fellow citizens. He then faced the jury. "Can't you see what these whores, coached by their infidel Arab lawyer, are doing? With their sob stories, they're winning your sympathy for them and the liberal left that they serve. If they win, we lose. They'll take our guns, restrict our hunting grounds, indoctrinate our schools with nothing but liberal ideas, flood our country with immigrants, like this Arab, who will vote for them. They are part of that women's movement that preaches, not just their equality with men, but the superiority of women, especially in the workplace and politics. Today, they're slandering me. Tomorrow, they'll be gunning for you." Mayor Molson turned from the jurors to glare at Judge Appleby. "Judge, I can't believe you would let your court stoop so low as to showcase such anti-American nonsense as this Arab is promoting."

Many observers in the gallery shouted their approval of their mayor's harangue. Several jurors nodded their heads in agreement. A high percentage of the locals resented immigrants, mistrusted Black people, feared government control and believed men, not women, should occupy leadership positions. People of opposing views shouted their slogans, each trying to be heard above the others on everything from abortion to zoo animals' rights.

In response, the judge brought down his gavel so furiously that the handle broke. "I'll have order in this court," he shouted, finally subduing the mayor-initiated mayhem. "If this occurs again, I'll find the offending parties in contempt of court, which carries the penalty of jail or a hefty fine. Now, Mr. Ahmad, please continue."

As Bashir turned to address the jury, Marta started sobbing.

"Enough disruption!" the judge exploded. "Mr. Ahmad, please calm your client."

"Marta, What...?"

"I felt a heavy dark cloud descend on us as everyone was spouting off his views in a mean-spirited, quarrelsome way," Marta said. "I saw what hate can do, dividing us from one another. I wished for someone to calm us-- a peacemaker to replace our hate with love for one another, or at least respect.

"But then I realized, 'How could I ask you all to give up your hate if I was unwilling to give up my hatred for the men who so cruelly treated me, who I swore I'd never forgive?' I justified my hate, because of the extreme cruelty certain men had inflicted on me. But now I see that as Jesus loved those who inflicted on him unimaginable cruelty, he wants me to join him in the peacemaking work of forgiveness. So, in this very moment I am letting go of my hatred; I am forgiving the men on the 'to be murdered' list I've carried for years."

Marta reached down into her bosom, removed, and unfolded a piece of paper that she at once began tearing into tiny shreds, which she dumped into a nearby waste basket. She turned then to Krystyl saying, "Now I see why you kept telling me to forgive. I feel so much lighter."

Marta grabbed Krystyl's hand, and said, "I join you in forgiving all who have abused us, some of whom are here in this room."

An incredible silence overcame the courtroom, as Marta and Krystyl looked around, at the men who had hurt them, with tearful eyes, spilling over with forgiveness. Some men ignored or ducked from their view. Others wiped their eyes.

"Objection!" the prosecutor protested. "This has nothing to do with the murder these women have committed!"

The judge, facing Bashir, said, "You asked me to let the jurors get to know Marta and Krystyl, which I did. I thought it to be necessary for overcoming the serious disadvantages the two faced due to the nature of their work. But we need to get on with this trial, so we refuse any more biographical details. So, unless either party has any other evidence to provide, it's time for the jury to deliberate."

#

I watched as Krystyl and Marta left the court room, while the jury deliberated, turning to the others, I exhaled deeply. "Wow! God just showed up, big time!"

"It was encouraging to see the power of forgiveness at work in Marta. Even if we win this trial, it won't top the loving way in which she looked with forgiveness on the men who most misused her."

"I agree, but it doesn't look like the trial is going our way. Until the mayor played his cards, I thought we had a chance," Bashir said as we filed out of the courtroom.

"What? I thought the mayor hurt his case by his outburst," I said.

"Ordinarily, such a tirade would hurt their cause," Bashir agreed, "but I saw jurors, who seemed to be against the mayor's corrupt leadership during the jury selection phase, nodding in agreement with the mayor's spiel. Such jurors would be biased against me, an Arab, and would see Krystyl and Marta as merely prostitutes, not as the amazingly transformed persons we had shown them to be. If I am guessing rightly, the best we can hope for is a hung jury."

"It is discouraging, but let's take fresh hope from our Lord who has encouraged me through a promise I found in my Bible reading this morning. In Psalm 46, God says he's a very present help in time of trouble," Bashir said. "This is certainly a troubling time and God has already shown up in Marta's gaining the power to forgive. How about the rest of us, can we all trust God's overpowering presence to be here the rest of this day?"

Everyone added their 'Amens', some more heartily than others.

#

We waited only an hour for the jury to decide. "Your Honor, it's obvious to this jury that we have people of unbending opinion. So, that means we're a hung jury."

We sat in stunned disbelief. "How could anyone not believe the truth of Krystyl's and Marta's stories? And the logic of Bashir's arguments?"

I was thrown into a tailspin of anger at the way things turned out: *"Was this the best that God could do?"*

As we waited to be dismissed, we heard a commotion. The door swung open and in walked a strikingly beautiful Black woman followed by reporters eager to get the scoop on Ana Grimes.

Once again, by my doubts, I had sold God short. I nudged Bashir. "That's Ana Grimes!"

"Your Honor," Bashir turned to the judge who was unbuttoning his robe. "Please advise us. What do we do when the one who is dead shows up in the court that's determining whether her death is suicide or homicide? May I present to you Ms. Ana Grimes. Since this trial is all about how she died, let's give her a chance to tell us."

Judge Appleby shook his head in disbelief as he re-buttoned his robe, "Court is in session. Proceed."

Bashir asked Ana to take the stand. "I'm Bashir Ahmad, your lawyer. This is my first time to represent someone from the dead, so let me catch my breath... Ana, please explain how it is that you are here and not in some watery grave," Bashir asked.

"I made it look like I was attached to the briefcase when I jumped. But I wasn't. I was just holding on to the briefcase. After it pulled me about ten feet beneath the surface, I let go of it. Then I swam underwater to the pilings that support the dock. I hid behind the pilings until all the police had left."

"Did you tell anyone of your plan to jump?" Bashir asked.

"No."

"Did anyone assist you in jumping?"

"No. These two tried to stop me." Ana pointed to Krystyl and Marta.

"Let it be noted that the charge of assisting suicide is invalid," Bashir said. "Sitting here, alive and well, is the one who supposedly drowned herself."

Epilogue

Our courageous Krystyl, Ana, and Marta spent a year in Adult and Teen Challenge's excellent rehab, taking Bible-based courses in how to overcome drug and sexual addiction.

I kept the promise I made to help Ana reunite with her family. Talk about confession and repentance! Ana chose to do it in her parent's church because most of the members had faithfully prayed for her. She asked forgiveness for the pain, anxiety, and shame she had brought on her family and the church. Everyone walked to the front of the church to hug and forgive her, joining her in joyous weeping.

The three women discovered a mutual love of singing and were welcomed in churches, service clubs, and schools, not only for their gripping story of escape from sexual slavery but also for their inspirational music.

To avoid familiar places where they had done drugs, and so-called friends, they took jobs at an Adult and Teen Challenge Center ninety miles from our city. They serve as counselors and office personnel.

Before they met Jesus, their pimps had forced them to expose their bodies to clients who shamefully abused them. Night after night, against their wills, they were caught naked, exposed to abuse and belittlement. Now, they are clothed in the security of God's love and the protection of his people. As the Bible says, they are clothed in Christ.

Romance? Not yet. Evil men have damaged their ability to feel safe, and to believe they are loved for their mental, social, and spiritual selves, not just their physical beauty. Krystyl has a friend who does love her for all that she is. And he is willing to wait until she can believe it. Marta is still trusting God for such a friend, and Ana seems to be content in her singleness. We'll see. God holds in high honor single people who serve him in ways married people cannot. But their singleness must be a gift of love for Christ, not the result of fear or disgust at the thought of being married.

#

Thanks to Al's organizing skills, a new political party called the Pure Pleasure Party was launched. Every precinct in the county has a captain. And every captain has materials that provide a thorough picture of sexploitation in our county, including missing persons thought to be abducted into sexual or economic slavery, for whom we urge people to be on the lookout.

"It is the perfect time for starting a new party," Al told me. "People are fed up with the empty promises of Republicans and Democrats as well as Conservatives and Liberals."

The PPP workers spend time in voters' homes explaining PPP positions and listening to concerns. We train our people to make no promises but show our concern by writing down people's issues and inviting them to our meetings where we discuss and pray and plan how to address each issue raised.

Many express surprise and appreciation for our including prayer as part of our meetings. Some question it. Very few flat out reject the idea. We simply tell people we want to bring God back into the shaping of our culture.

We make no apologies for prayer. Our country needs all the help we can get, so why not seek the help of the One whose record shows that he has mightily delivered nations from destruction? He can do the same for us.

I wish I could report that all is turning out well for the new party. But precisely because the PPP has been so successful, they have received significant push back, Al became the first martyr for the PPP cause. At least it looks like his death was punishment for his work against the police chief and mayor. Through careful, methodical investigation, Al gathered enough evidence to put Mayor Molson and Police Chief Alexander in prison for selling child pornography and for sexual abuse of minors. The evidence Al gathered left no hiding place for the police chief and mayor. They were caught naked.

Of the five police officers who testified against the chief, two have 'accidentally' met untimely deaths. Suspicious, to say the least.

#

Remember Ron? The fiftyish, well-read firefighter who inspired me to do what's right even if it's hard, very hard. Remember how he motivated me by telling me of heroes in Black History— Henry Box Brown and Dred Scott? Well, after Al's death, Ron took leadership of the Pure Pleasure Party. When told that he was carrying out all that Al had envisioned, Ron said, "The way I see it, this is not merely Al or me, it's from the Lord, and it's marvelous...."

#

Then there's Pete, Ron's sidekick, and bodyguard. He's using more and more of his retirement to help Ron. Pete's three sons volunteer their expertise to the PPP. Pete's youngest son, like Al, is gifted with organizational skills that PPP needs, especially if the party goes state-wide, then national.

#

Occasionally, we hear rumors of Mac and Fly Guy. Two guys who look like them were reported to have been big spenders in saloons and gambling joints in northern Mexico. The latest rumor has them languishing in a Mexican jail after Mac is said to have broken a man's neck in a bar-room brawl. Who knows? The wise man, Moses, said, "be sure your sin will find you out." If not today, then some very soon tomorrow, Mac and Fly Guy will be caught naked too.

#

Joe Coleman, the police officer, who offered to us his home on the river and who turned out to be a spy sent by the police chief, was so convinced of the chief's wrongdoing that he became one of those who testified against the chief. He was also one of the men who died mysteriously, along with Al.

The mysterious deaths have ceased. They backfired. They were intended to frighten us. Instead, they increased the loyalty and courage of PPP members. Intended to express revenge, they evoked love.

#

Heather finally gathered the compassion and courage needed to go with me to talk with her stepdad. But he took her heartfelt forgiveness as an insult. "I don't need your forgiveness," he yelled.

"But Dad, you said the family would be better off if I had succeeded in committing suicide."

"That's still true." He yelled, reaching for something behind him.

My hand went automatically to the gun at my hip when, at the same moment, the barrel of his Beretta 92 pistol appeared. We were sitting at a standoff with our sights pointed across the table at each other.

Then he angled his gun into Heather's face. "First, I'm going to shoot Heather... for listening to you, Mr. Van Moeller... and then I'm going to shoot you for the shit you've been feeding her about loving her neighbor. That's the kind of weak stuff that tells me you're all show and don't have the balls to shoot me."

I made a quick pivot and fired. I missed. I was trying to knock the gun out of his hand. Instead, I hit the radial artery in his wrist. Blood gushed out. I ripped off my shirt, starting to twist it around his upper arm. He bit my forearm. I hit him hard, knocking him out. With him unconscious, we wrapped the tourniquet tightly. The blood flow slowed to a trickle. An ambulance responded to our 911 appeal and led us to the hospital. As they wheeled him off to the ER, I warned the medical staff of his unpredictability. I waited in the hall. Heather waited beside his bed.

"The wound is too large and complicated to fix with stitches," the doc said. "We have to do surgery."

Ms. Osborne met us in the hallway.

We let her know all that we had said and done, including Hank's threatening to kill Heather.

"That's Hank," Heather's mom said, shaking her head. "Always right. Never once has he admitted he was wrong."

"But has he ever pulled a gun on his daughter and threatened to kill her?" I asked.

"Yes, but I didn't think he'd ever go through with it," Heather's mom said.

I rolled my eyes and bit my tongue. *How sick! To gamble with your own child's life.*

#

As we were driving home, I explained the narcissistic personality disorder to Heather. "Your stepdad seems to fit that disorder. He thinks he's superior to everyone. He won't listen to anyone unless that person confirms his viewpoint."

I wanted her to think about who she lets define her. Should it be Jesus or her murderously irrational stepdad? "I hope you listen to what Jesus says about you, not to what your sick stepdad calls you.

"The Bible describes who you really are. Jesus calls us his bride, his beloved, and his friend. We are a part of his body. We fellow believers belong to Jesus and to one another."

"I know in my head that I shouldn't let him define me," Heather said. "But when I feel low, Dad's angry voice haunts me. Jesus' voice seems small and distant."

"That's when it's good to have friends say to us what Jesus would say. And what he would say right now, along with a big hug is: 'I'm so glad you are in my family, Heather.'"

#

The hospital nursing staff put up with Hank's flirting and bullying for two days, then sent him home a day early because he was so difficult. Before dismissing him, a hospital social worker learned from Mrs. Osborne that he was even more mean and bullying at home.

"You need to think about removing yourself and your children from Mr. Osborne. He's a dangerous man," the nurse pleaded.

Mrs. Osborne took the warning seriously and arranged with the shelter for battered women.

Hank had been home only an hour, when Heather's sister called, saying that Mrs. Osborne told Hank she and her daughter were leaving him. Hank went into a rage and threatened suicide."

Mrs. Osborne and her daughter (Heather's younger sister) took the family car and were on their way to a shelter for abused women, when Hank called, pleading with them to return. They told Hank he was well-provided for, and from this moment on they would cut off communication. That's when he again threatened suicide. Mrs. Osborne answered him by hanging up. Heather's younger sister then called us, and I took the phone.

"We've got a problem," the sister said.

"So, where's the trouble?" I asked her.

"Mom has pulled into a gas station halfway to the women's shelter. She's second-guessing her move."

"What did you tell her?" I asked.

"I wanted to tell her he was manipulating her, but I thought she would take it better from you or Heather. Would one of you call her cell phone right now?"

Which I did.

"I'm so scared," Mrs. Osborne repeatedly whimpered.

"What are you afraid of, Mrs. Osborne?" I asked.

"That he'll do it."

"Has he threatened suicide before?" I asked.

"Five or six times."

"Why did he threaten to do it back then?"

"To get me to do something I didn't want to do."

"So back then it was just a way of manipulating you, right?" I asked.

"That's what my counselor said, too. Both of you say he's manipulating me by threatening something horrible."

"What do you think?"

"He is a manipulator... But...."

"But what if this time it's for real?" I asked. "Is that what you're asking?"

"Yes."

"What will it tell him if you give in to this threat and go back home?" I asked.

"I can be controlled by threats?" she said.

"Is that what you want to tell him?" I asked. "I'm your little puppet. You can manipulate me to do anything if you threaten me. Do you want to say that to him?"

"That is what I've been saying to him, isn't it?" she said.

"Do you want to stop telling him he can control you by threats?" I asked. "If so, when?"

"Now." I heard her starting the car. "I'm headed for the shelter. Thank you."

I haven't let go of my dream of Hank radically changed by a humbling encounter with Jesus and then reconciled with his family. As long as Hank is alive there is hope.

#

Jenna took Heather into our home as a soul sister. They were sixteen when Heather came to live with us. They both loved to read.

Jenna introduced Heather to Tolkien's *Lord of the Rings*, C. S. Lewis' *Chronicles of Narnia* and *Mere Christianity*, Charles Dickens' *Tale of Two Cities*, and George Macdonald's *The Princess and Curdie*.

Heather introduced Jenna to *Anne Frank's Diary of a Young Girl*, Harper Lee's *To Kill a Mockingbird*, and George Orwell's *1984*.

Morally healthy people need more than good books. We need to have a cause to live for, and we need people, preferably quite different from us, to work with, serve, and learn from. Heather and Jenna volunteer at the local Adult and Teen Challenge Center. They provide delicious snacks for the residents and a shoulder to cry on.

And when the Pure Pleasure Party needs help, Heather and Jenna are often the first to volunteer. As budding journalists, they write articles, design leaflets, and are starting on a book titled *Caught Covered*.

# #

Caught Naked could describe us all. Just as we cover our private parts, so we all have parts of our lives that we keep private, covered, unmentioned. I could wax eloquent on the virtue of keeping these things hidden from all (except for a wise friend who will keep private what is spoken in confidence and treat it with tender reverence).

I am troubled by the 'tell-all' interviews on some TV shows. Social media provides another venue that shows and tells too much. When celebrities or ordinary people let the entire world know their lusts, phobias, and the things they despise, they spread out for all the world to see what should only be entrusted to a loyal friend. Then they wonder why people caustically criticize and unfairly judge them. I have found the world to be a mixed bag of prejudiced, foolish, hateful, wise, loving, and compassionate people. Do yourself a favor. If you need help in understanding your inner self, search out a gifted counselor who is wise and loving. Stop casting your pearls before swine.

We all need hidden places that we reserve for God alone to review with us. Those hidden places cover broken pieces of our lives that hurt too much to uncover and understand. Or they protect incredibly beautiful experiences that we haven't found words to describe. So, we wait on God to tell us when, if ever, we can share those experiences. Meanwhile, we contentedly keep secret what should remain private.

Having said that, I hasten to say we sometimes keep secret what should be made known. God has ways of revealing those things, embarrassing as they might be. It's as if we are caught naked. And that's good. God allows us to be disrobed so that his healing servants can better see what is sick, damaged, and toxic.

Mac and Fly Guy were caught naked, but they refused to take a good look at themselves. Instead, they ran.

You could say that Heather, Krystyl, Ana, and Marta were caught naked. Or to be more exact, they were forced to uncover themselves. Their physical nakedness pointed to their even more devastating nakedness of soul and spirit. These women took a long look at themselves in contrast to Jesus Christ. They liked what they saw in Jesus. They drew close to him and trusted him to transform them to be more like him. He is doing that, so their inward beauty is more stunning than their outward beauty.

#

Speaking of transforming grace, Boris... Do you remember Boris? He was the guard at the brothel south of town. Remember? Jenna shot him in the back, paralyzing him from the waist down. Well, Jenna visited him every Sunday afternoon for a while. During the first visits, he let loose with an ear-popping eruption of expletives that turned the room blue with his hatred for her. Jenna just smiled and gave him a cookie or some fudge. She'd say something like, "Jesus told me to make this for you. I hope you like it." Then she'd leave.

This went on for two months. Jenna found out that no one came to visit Boris. That made her even more determined to visit him. Then came the Sunday when Boris asked Jenna, "Why do you keep coming to see me despite my screaming at you?"

"Jesus wants you to have visitors," Jenna answered. She opened her Bible to chapter twenty-five of Matthew where Jesus says we should visit those who are sick and in prison. "I'm just doing what Jesus told me to do."

To shorten a long story, Boris accepted Jesus as his Savior and friend. The nurses say his attitude has mysteriously changed. "If not for my injury, I might never have met Jesus. And I'd rather have him than to be able to walk," Boris says.

Jenna wheels Boris to churches, service clubs, and school assemblies in his wheelchair. Everywhere they go, they talk about loving your enemies, forgiving the one who has most deeply hurt you, and finding the best in the worst. Boris explains his continual happiness by saying, "I never had a friend until Jenna. Now I've got Jenna and all her friends, plus Jesus. How could I not be happy?"

#

Last and probably least is the guy who fished Heather's note out of the storm sewer on a rainy night. If it weren't for Heather's cry for help and my clumsy response, where would

Heather be? Krystyl? Marta? Ana? Boris? Pete? Ron? Joe? Heather's mother? Where would I be? and my wife, Kate?

By the way, I, too, was caught naked, more than once. Perhaps the most embarrassing example came early on when I couldn't hide from Heather my lustful desire for Krystyl's massage. I'm glad now that Heather blew my cover. It made me realize I needed to fortify my devotion to my wife. She, knowing how easily distracted I can be, how hard it is to reserve my eyes for her and her alone... She mounts a guard over my TV, social media, and movie viewing. And, of course, by making sure life doesn't get too boring, she helps immensely.

Caught Naked Discussion Guide

Most of these questions are open-ended, having no 'correct' answer. They are intended to evoke serious thinking.

1. The cry for "Help!" launched Dave into a dangerous, daring adventure. Regardless of how you might think of Dave's way of trying to help a person in trouble, what's commendable in his response to the girl's situation [Chapter 1]?

2. Is your life boring, lacking adventure, or too ordinary? Could it be due to your fear of the unusual, the risky, or the unscheduled? What beliefs, attitudes, behaviors bring adventure to your life? Does being adventuresome, fun-loving, creative, and having friends with whom you enjoy life contribute to being a wholesome person ?

3. As he goes through suffering at the hands of sex traffickers, Dave reflects on his own involvement in the sex trade: As I lay writhing on the cold concrete floor, I wondered, *how many of the girls I've looked at in porn pictures and videos were trained to expose and sell their bodies as Mac and Fly Guy were 'training' the teen girl I had rescued?* What is Dave beginning to realize [Chapter 1]?

4. What do you think of Ron's, the Black fireman's, attitude and actions toward the racist cop who threatened harm to him and his family [Chapter 2]? What role does racism play in sexual exploitation?

5. Dave likens the sex traffickers to "predators… like a pack of wolves. They hunt down, trap, and tear people apart [as Mac and his partner were trying to dehumanize the girl they had

spread-eagled]. For selfish pleasure and profit, they trample and smear their filth on innocent victims like that girl… how can they do it? I asked Ron this question that had pursued me since my early days on the police force. "In my line of work, I see the tragic effects of evil men and women up close every day. And none of the answers gives a lasting solution," Ron said. "The questions rise again tomorrow, just as soul-searching and scary as ever."

Precisely. I thought. *For the first time, I've found someone who understands.* What evils do you find to be beyond understanding? Is sex trafficking one of them? If so, why? If not, why not? When you struggle with extremely difficult issues, what is it like when you find someone who understands [Chapter 3]?

6. Dave said he was like a sex predator, when in his thoughts he used women for his pleasure, when he took them apart – enjoying their breasts, their thighs, their legs, instead of seeing them as whole persons and appreciating them for all that God has made them to be. Does Dave's description show ways in which perhaps you have been viewing others wrongly [Chapter 4]?

7. Dave and Ron talked about the difference between fighting skirmishes and an all-out war against sex trafficking. Is it skirmishes or all-out war in your village or city? What could you do to make it a well-coordinated, and ongoing battle, rather than a fight here and a fight there [Chapter 5]?

8. Years earlier, Dave had visited adult bookstores, gentlemen's clubs, and their ilk out of curiosity, which swiftly led him into

addiction to porn. He hadn't frequented porn sites for thirty years because Jesus had delivered him from that addiction. Yet he felt the same craving as he did back then. After all these years of sobriety, he was deep in the spider's web [Chapter 7]. Addiction counselors teach that if you return to an addiction, you don't return to a beginning stage. You return to the stage you were at when you put the addiction aside. Is it true? What safeguards do you need to establish to help you prevent going back to where you left off?

9. Chapter 7 describes sexual temptation as feeling a rush— that combination of intense physical desire with mental numbness, and spiritual blackout. In this scenario you allow desire to be all-powerful. It stings the mind-- numbing it-- meaning you stop thinking, or you stop thinking clearly when you flirt with sexual temptation. And you lose all awareness of God. Have you been there, done that? How do you reverse or undo sexual temptation?

10. Dave invites Heather, who had been spreadeagled and repeatedly raped, to live with his family while getting back to normal. She responds, "There is no getting back to normal after what I've been through [Chapter 9]." Is Heather doomed to be spoiled goods forever? Can she be the 16-year-old she used to be? Will the abuse from her stepfather and Mac and Fly Guy forever haunt her? In what ways can her horrible experiences make her a uniquely better woman?

11. Heather waxes eloquent as she describes the darkness of our existence. She wonders where God is in the darkness [Chapter

9]. How would you respond to Heather? What do you think of Dave's response?

12. Which of the seven temptation blockers do you find most doable [Chapter 10]?

13. Dave told Mac a partly true, but misleading, story in his attempt to free Heather [Chapters 11 and 12]. Are there biblical examples of this kind of deception? What are your thoughts about this?

14. It seemed that the first woman Dave tried to rescue from the fire was so entrenched in and emotionally damaged by the lie she was forced to live that she yielded to its damning conclusion [Chapter 13]. Reflect on the emotional, spiritual, and physical damages that people abused by sexploitation suffer.

15. When trying to explain how everyone kept going, Dave asked if it were God or adrenaline [Chapter 13]. What do you think?

16. Dave questions why he feels freer from sexual temptation in his relationship with Heather compared to the other women [Chapter 14]. He thinks it's because he's closer to Heather. It's as if she were his daughter. And just as there's a taboo against sexualizing the relationship of a biological father and daughter, so there's a kind of taboo against sexualizing the relationship with one whom you consider being your daughter, sister, mother, or father. Could this taboo be what Paul is alluding to in 1 Timothy 5:2? where he says, "treat younger women as sisters." Is this concept helpful to you? Explain.

17a. In a scene from Chapter 15, Krystyl came up to me and ran her fingers softly down my arm. "Why not [sleep] with us?" Krystyl sounded almost seductive. "We could give you the ultimate massage and send you off to the sweetest sleep you've ever had. You deserve it after all you've done for us." ...*She's offering sex as if it were a normal way to say thank you.* My brain froze. Animal instinct usurped my will. Torrents of desire smashed all my taboos. I would have yielded like a bull in heat if it weren't for that 'how-could-you?' look Heather gave me. That piercing glare unlocked my brain; I could think again. I could question—*what am I, man or beast?* I could remember how demeaning and enslaving it was to be controlled by sex and how uplifting and freeing it is to have Christ in control of my passions. I was free—to be what I was created to be. I was free to be faithful to my wife and to show these women the goodness of faithfulness. So, I ignored Krystyl's offer. Dave was at the point of surrender to sexual temptation. He had stopped thinking. What else is characteristic of a man ready to take the plunge? What brought him to a screeching halt?

17b. What is characteristic of a person who overcomes sexual temptation?

The answer to this question is so crucial that I am going to supply it—.

You must THINK! Think about what you'd be doing to yourself, your family, your friends, co-workers, your church. List other damages that could result from your yielding to this powerful temptation. Think! Is it worth the damage it will cause? Someone might say that he did it in secret, so no one will be hurt. But God sees all, and he is the last person I'd want to offend, after all the kindness he has shown me.

18. Dave, a retired police officer, automatically packs a gun when he thinks he's heading into danger. Never does Dave shoot to kill. And he has rigorously trained himself to shoot accurately, to shoot only to prevent another from harming or killing. Are guns a reliable way to social change? What do you think of Jenna's motive for shooting Boris?

19. In Chapters 22 through 26, Ron summarizes the story of his life. So does Heather, Marta, Krystyl, and Ana. What does each of these stories have in common? What are some major differences in these persons' lives? What impresses you the most in these stories?

20. In Chapters 27 and 28, the women do handcrafts and exercises while the men discuss how to battle sex trafficking. Which is more important?

21. The men, except for Joe, commit themselves to all-out war against sex trafficking. What would make someone want to do that [Chapter 28]?

22. Demons had controlled Krystyl for years, but Krystyl thought Jesus had cast them out. Not willing to lose her, the demons came back to test if she belonged to Satan or Jesus. Once again, the demons were exorcised. And Krystyl experienced thorough healing, which she described in this way. "I felt wrenching pain as they departed, but it was as if Jesus' hands were touching me, finding every wound, and healing all of me that had been damaged." ... What kind of powers are we

up against? Read Ephesians 6:12-17. How can we win this battle?

23. Quitting drugs cold turkey as Ana, Marta, and Krystyl did is extremely risky. Why do most people addicted to drugs, including Christians, need medicine to help them through withdrawal? Do all harmful habits disappear when Christ makes us new creatures? [Explain.] Why doesn't God free us immediately from all harmful habits?

24. How do you feel when someone you have been helping in their walk with Jesus skips out on you? Karen and Dave didn't give up. They waited and prayed. And soon they were back in touch with two of the three who had seemingly rejected their counsel. When someone 'disappears,' what might it mean other than rejection?

25. In Chapter 32, Dave makes up a lighthearted, self-deprecating poem that warns people not to do what he did:

Stop looking back with fear.

Instead, look ahead with cheer.

In the darkness don't grope.

Take Christ's hand and hope....

How might humor, especially self-deprecating humor, help encourage people like our friends? Is the message of Dave's poem relevant to the needs of Marta, Krystyl, and Ana? If so, how so?

26. After Ana drowned herself, a cop kept shooting into the place where she jumped. Angered, Krystal told the cop: "You got one thing right. Being a slut is worse than shit. That's why they mocked Jesus, because so many of his friends, if not sluts, were shitty. Jesus welcomed these people. But he didn't stop there. He made them new. He's doing that for me. He'll do that for you. Why were shitty people and sluts attracted to Jesus?

27. Chapter 34 shows Jenna struggling with vengeful thoughts toward those who sexually exploit others.

How was her conflict resolved? What do you think of the ways she resolved it. Comment especially on the paragraph that begins with this sentence: Because to take revenge you have to judge that a person deserves punishment and that you're the one who should punish him.

28. In the earlier part of Chapter 35, Dave confronts the police chief, describing changes the chief should make.

In the latter part of Chapter 35, Karen, Jenna, and Heather provide drinks for the police who have harassed them. Is that wise? Explain how both Dave's honest confronting and Karen's kindness could be beneficial to their cause?

29. What helped Dave to not give in to the seductive messages piped into his jail cell?

30. One theme of this story is that adversity is the pathway to blessings that never come without the adversity. We see that theme again in Chapter 38 when Dave is thrown into prison with inmates who beat Dave to within an inch of his life because

his excellent detective work landed six of them in prison. But that puts him in the prison hospital from which he can and does escape. In what other situations in this book do hard times bring good results? Why?

31. Chapters 39 and 41 describe our friends' all-out effort to free those who were held captive by sex trafficking. In the U.S. one way the people speak is through their political parties or, at least, they try to. If no party champions their causes, they can start a new party. Rarely does that new party gain a following that competes with the established parties. Do you think the Pure Pleasure political party will succeed? Why or why not?

32. The major characters in this story are fighting sexual exploitation through a multifaceted community campaign with a major emphasis on politics. Maybe politics does not interest you. Enter 'fighting sex exploitation' into your browser to find organizations devoted to fighting sexual exploitation. As you read through the descriptions of what these organizations do, the Holy Spirit just might say, "This one is for you." That will be the cry for "Help!" And so begins your venture.

Other Books by Doug Weeks

Adventure trilogy...

Children of the Night

Search for the Scroll

Circle of Seven

for pre-teens of all ages.

A spry old man, Apostle John, exiled to the Isle of Patmos, writes a message to seven churches in nearby Turkey. Thirteen-year-old Apollos with his younger sister join the beloved old man for high adventure evoked by John's mysterious message.

Available at Amazon.

Search for Douglas Wesley Weeks in Amazon under "books."

#

On My Journey Home

Author's memoir

Available at Amazon.

Search for D. Wesley Weeks in Amazon under "books."

Afterword

Join the fight against sex trafficking by checking out the following:

- Jaco Booyens' sister was sex-trafficked for six years. Through feature films and other media Jaco tells his sister's saga and the stories of many others who were stripped of their humanity, hated themselves, attemtpted suicide, and felt forever ruined. Type **Jaco Booyens** into your search engine.

- Search *Enough is Enough's anti-pornography campaigns* to make the internet safe for children.

- To demolish a business, take away its customers. Most users of illicit sexual services are sex addicts. Heal the addict and you take away a customer. Through its 220 North American residential centers, *Adult and Teen Challenge* operates a*n extraordinarily successful* ministry of overcoming addictions, including sexual addiction.

- For a powerful ministry to women, check out *Home ministry* led by Beth Greco. Reach her at bgreco@home.com.

- If none of the above fits, Wikipedia has a lengthy list of organizations fighting sex trafficking.